AS A SHIELD

A Davis Morgan Mystery

AS A SHIELD

A Davis Morgan Mystery

Danny Pelfrey
Wanda Pelfrey

DANNY & WANDA PELFREY

CROSSLINK
PUBLISHING

As A Shield: A Davis Morgan Mystery

P
C CrossLink Publishing
www.crosslinkpublishing.com

ISBN 978-1-63357-091-7

Library of Congress Control Number: 2016955098

Scripture quotations are taken from THE HOLY BIBLE, NEW INTERNATIONAL VERSION®, NIV® Copyright© 1973, 1978, 1984, 2011 by Biblica, Inc.™ Used by permission. All rights reserved worldwide.

This book is a work of fiction. Names, characters, businesses, organizations, places, events and incidents either are the product of the author's imagination or are used fictitiously. Any resemblance to actual persons, living or dead, events, or locales is entirely coincidental.

ACKNOWLEDGEMENTS

We would be remiss if we did not acknowledge some people who played an important part in making AS A SHIELD a reality. Carol Crawford of Blue Ridge Georgia did major editing. While we have forever read and loved fiction, especially mystery, our writing background is nonfiction. Carol helped teach us some critical basics.

A lot of technical knowledge is required to take a book from conception to a published work in today's world. Our son-in-law, Jason Dailey, was free with his time and expertise in patiently walking us through those sometimes confusing details. Our friend Julie Stephens helped us in making decisions and setting up the social media needed to promote our work. We thank both of them for helping bring us into the twenty-first century regarding things technical.

Then most of all we owe a great debt to the people of Adairsville, Georgia, who are the inspiration for *AS A SHIELD*. Their contribution started long before our book was in our minds and will, no doubt, continue for the rest of our lives.

The Adairsville News   *August 7, 1917*

SKELETONS DISCOVERED IN ADAIRSVILLE CAVE

Adairsville, Georgia, August 4, 1917 – Mr. Samuel Ammon and his neighbor, Frank Evans, made a startling discovery recently while digging in a cave located in Ammon's farm. According to reports, the two farmers, while attempting to increase the size of the passage between two chambers, uncovered what appeared to be eighteen sets of human bones. The cave, which during the Civil War was sometimes used as a hiding place for valuables when Federal troops passed through the area, has long been a popular attraction, especially among young people.

Local doctor Dick Bradley confirmed that the relics are indeed human bones, but could not positively say of what race or how long they had lain in the cave. The Ammon farm is located a few miles from Adairsville near the Cedar Creek/Folsom community.

CHAPTER 1

There were still a few minutes of daylight left when the former preacher turned bookseller parked his new Jeep in the Adairsville Police Department lot. Davis Morgan had been chaplain for only a couple of weeks. One neat perk for Davis was that Chief Hanson allowed him, under normal circumstances, to accompany the officers when they patrolled the little North Georgia town. It was his friend Charley Nelson with whom Davis most enjoyed riding, and Charley recently told him he appreciated the company.

Even before Davis stepped out of his vehicle, Charley rushed out the front door on his way to the patrol car parked in the lot beside the Methodist Church Annex.

"I saw you drive up," the tanned young policeman said as he hurried toward his assigned automobile.

"You can't wait to get into that patrol car, can you? I suspect that would be your permanent home if the chief would allow it." Davis walked rapidly to keep up with the young officer who always moved as if he were on his way to a fire.

"It's true I'm more at home there than anywhere else. What can I say? I love my job."

Charley got into the car at the same time Davis opened the door on the opposite side. He slid into the passenger seat and buckled his seatbelt. "It looks like a storm is brewing." Charley looked up toward the sky where dark heavy clouds were rapidly coming together. The rain began to fall even before they drove out of the parking lot, at first lightly, but by the time they got to the traffic light at highways 140 and 41, the rain fell hard, while the trees bent in the wind. Charley headed east on 140 toward the Interstate 75 ramp. "It'll be a busy night if this keeps up," he remarked, squinting.

Lighting lit up the sky now at regular intervals, with each flash followed by a loud blast of thunder. The wipers, slashing rapidly across the windshield, could not keep up with the rain. Davis worried that Charley would be unable to see the centerline on the road. Then suddenly hail was falling.

"Those may be the biggest hailstones I've ever seen." There was concern in Davis's voice. The pounding on the windshield made him uneasy. He was afraid the glass wouldn't stand up against such punishment.

"We had better get off the road." Charley waited for a westbound car to pass before he turned his own vehicle left toward the QT station. They pulled into a parking space beside the store to wait out the storm. "I haven't seen a storm like this since our tornado a few years back."

At the mention of the tornado, Davis looked straight ahead and became quiet. That tornado did more than a little damage to their town just four years earlier. Amy and Jay were now on their way to Marietta for dinner; he hoped they would be safe.

They will be all right, he told himself. Davis had memorized a significant amount of scripture, and he found comfort that it was always there when needed. It was a verse from Psalm 5:12 that came to his mind now.

For surely, O Lord, you bless the righteous; you surround them with your favor as with a shield.

He offered a silent prayer for the safety of his daughter and future son-in-law. When he put his daughter's welfare in the hands of the Lord, he immediately experienced a sense of calmness. Davis also said a brief prayer for his friend Charley who he knew was not among the *righteous*. The nasty weather would make his night a difficult one.

The two unlikely friends made conversation for a time while they waited for the storm to subside. "I need only a few more hours with my instructor before I'll be ready to solo. When I get my license I will take you up for a real ride high in the sky. That is if you're not afraid to go up with me."

"Why would I be afraid of flying with a licensed pilot?" Actually, Davis felt his mouth go dry at the thought of being a passenger in a small aircraft guided by the sometimes daring young policeman. "I didn't know you were that close to having your pilot's license."

"I've spent almost all of my spare time in the air over the past few weeks. I really enjoy being up there. I'm anxious to get on with it. Someday I would like to have my own plane, but I doubt that will happen as long as I depend on a cop's paycheck. Maybe I could earn more money if I were to become a big-time author like you." Charley was aware of Davis's assignment to write a book on local history and liked to rib him about it.

"Your paycheck could be sufficient if you would cut out some of the nightlife and save some of the money you spend on...."

At that moment the radio crackled to life. Davis stopped short.

The department dispatcher spoke through the static. "Charley, we just got a report that a fallen tree brought down a power line out on Woody Road. I contacted Georgia Power, but you had better get out there to direct traffic before someone gets hurt."

"Katie, where exactly on Woody Road is the tree?" Charley spoke into the mike.

"It's west of the railroad about halfway down the hill before you get to the bridge. Be careful. There have been some reports of tornadoes touching down at various places near here. Already we have dispatched three officers to accidents."

"We're on it," Charley assured the dispatcher. The policeman started the engine before he wheeled out of the parking lot with lights flashing to travel west toward Highway 41 where he turned right and then drove for a quarter of a mile to swerve left onto Woody Road at the Oothcalooga Baptist Church. From there they rode until they saw the large oak tree lying across the road with a broken power line tangled in its limbs. Charley parked the car just off the road. He was careful not to get stuck in the mud or get too close to the deep drop-off to their right.

"You stay in the car!" Charley barked before he stepped out to open the trunk to take out four orange cones. The rain dripped from his uniform cap into his face while he placed two of the cones on the road to stop the westbound traffic. The young officer then carefully made his way to the other side of the fallen oak to place cones in position to keep drivers who approached from that direction, away from the danger of the downed lines.

Davis watched the activity from his comfortable dry seat in the patrol car while Charley walked to the edge of the road and shone his flashlight on the gully. He squinted, leaned forward, and, immediately, to Davis's astonishment, he vanished. He had gotten too close to the edge and gone sliding into the woods below.

"Charley!" Davis shouted when he jumped from the car to run toward the spot. "Charley, are you okay?" In seconds, Davis was soaked to the skin. He could see nothing when he looked into the ravine. Not only was the darkness a problem, but the rain ran down his face into his eyes. "Charley are you hurt?" He cried out to his friend, trying his best to catch at least a glimpse of some movement below.

Then he heard Charley's voice. "You had better come down here, Davis. Be careful! The bank is steep and slick, but if you're careful you can make it. I need your help!"

Davis slowly made his descent to the bottom of the hill. He wished he had worn sneakers or at least footwear different from his leather-soled shoes that seemed to slip with every step he took. Not only did the mud make every step difficult, but the wet pine straw on the steep surface also proved to be a hazard. When he got to the bottom of the gully, he saw Charley on his knees in the mud. Then there was a moment of panic. He stopped in his tracks in shock at what was before him. "Not again," he mumbled, intensely focused on the sight before him. *Not again.*

Charley turned his head toward the horrified former preacher with a pained look on his face. "He's dead!" Charley, whose uniform was pretty much covered with Georgia red clay, tried to stand but stumbled at the effort, falling again to one knee. "Help me up the hill to the radio. I need to call the chief, but I think I sprained my ankle when I fell down that bank. It's not easy for me to walk."

The stunned police chaplain's mind flashed back to a few weeks previously when he discovered handyman Ed Hagan's battered body. As a pastor, he had several times been with people when they passed from life to death. He even had held the hand of a couple of them when they drew their last breath. He was once the first person on the scene after an automobile accident in which three people died, but never an ordeal like this—two bodies from separate incidents in such a short time span. He helped Charley to his feet, and supported him by putting his right arm across his back with his hand just under the injured policeman's arm. He timidly asked, "Was he murdered?"

"No. He died of natural causes."

"How do you know that?" Davis tried to support the policeman when he attempted to walk but found he wasn't very successful, so they stopped for a moment to allow him to readjust his hold.

"Look at him," Charley suggested. "What do you see?"

Davis looked closely at the body on the ground face up. "He looks like a middle-aged male perhaps a little beyond medium size with tattoos up and down both arms."

"Actually, if you were to pull his shirt up, you would find his body is pretty much covered with tattoos," Charley told him. "We got word from Doug at the funeral home this morning that the body of a man who died of natural causes at one of the motels near the highway had been stolen during the night. He described him as a middle-aged man with dark hair whose body is covered with tattoos. Our corpse seems to fit that description."

"I don't think there is any way I can give you enough support to make it straight up that hill. We will have to walk a piece further down the path where the ground is level with the road. Then we can make our way back up the pavement to the car."

The two men hobbled along the edge of the creek. With the help of Charley's flashlight, they found a good spot to make their way through the bushes to the road to finally get back to the car. By this time Davis was winded from supporting the weight of his friend, but had enough breath left to ask the question that had been on his mind for several minutes, "Why would anyone steal a body from the funeral home?"

"I don't have the slightest idea," Charley told him while opening the door of the patrol car to reach in for the radio mike.

"Katie, tell the chief I found that lost body. It is out here on Woody Road where the power lines are down. We'll be waiting for him."

After a moment the dispatcher responded, "He and Jed are already on their way. They should be there in about five minutes."

The Georgia Power truck pulled in behind the patrol car.

"You will have to wait a while before you start your cleanup," Charley informed them. "The chief will be here in a couple of minutes. He'll explain."

Moments later Chief Hanson, along with one of his officers, both in orange rain gear, appeared.

"Morgan, I should have known you would be nearby if there happened to be a body anywhere in the vicinity." The police chief stared in Davis's direction. Davis grinned but remained silent when the chief and his assistant, Jed, moved over to where Charley stood. They talked for a couple of minutes in tones Davis could not hear. Hanson and the officer he brought with him then went down the hill.

Charley hopped over to where Davis was stationed and suggested they both get into the patrol car. He then took a blanket from the car trunk to spread over the driver's seat before he seated himself on the blanket. Davis looked at him with an expression that silently asked, *What about me? Is it okay for me in my wet clothes to sit in this other seat?*

"It's okay—I'm muddy, you're just wet. Sit down, you can't damage that seat."

Davis and Charley remained in the patrol car while the two policemen who had gone down the hillside obviously searched the area. After an hour or so had passed, an ambulance from the funeral home arrived. Jim, an employee of the local institution who Davis knew well, along with another man he did not recognize, got out of the oversized vehicle. The chief gave directions that enabled Jim and his coworker to make their way down the hill to the spot where the body of the tattooed man lay in the mud. The two attendants returned in a few minutes with the corpse on a stretcher which was placed in the ambulance through the rear door.

The four-man Georgia power crew remained on sight to clean up the fallen tree and repair the power line. Chief Hanson with Jed stayed to direct traffic; the chief also sent Charlie and Davis home.

Charley did not let on if driving with the sprained ankle caused him any pain, but Davis knew Charley well enough to know he would rather suffer than allow someone else drive his patrol car.

On the way back to the police station where Davis would retrieve his Jeep, he and Charley discussed their evening. "What do you know about the man we found?" Davis questioned. "Is he local? With all those tattoos, I think I would remember him if I had seen him before."

"I know nothing about him, but I will after tomorrow." Charley continued, "The fact he died at the motel is probably a pretty good indication he is not local. I will go by the funeral home when they open tomorrow to take some pictures of his tattoos and question whoever is there. Then I plan to go to the motel to learn as much about him as possible."

"Why do you want pictures of his tattoos?" Davis probed with a puzzled expression. Charley pulled into the space beside where the red Jeep was parked.

"You wouldn't believe how much you can learn about a man from his tattoos. There was a recent case solved in Macon primarily from clues from the victim's tattoos. Remind me to sometime tell you the whole story."

"That makes sense. I guess you have to be careful to look at the minute as well as the obvious when there is a mystery. I'll talk with you tomorrow. Let me know what you learn about our tattooed man. Thanks for another wonderful evening," Davis facetiously added before he got out of the patrol car.

The bookseller who was coming to the end of what had been a very long day sighed and looked closely at the exterior of his new Jeep before he opened the door to get in. He hoped the storm had left no dents in the vehicle of his dreams which he had finally purchased last week even though it severely strained his budget. He could see no damage, but the light was not bright enough to get a good look. *I'll give it a good once-over in the morning,* he told himself. He relaxed when he saw that Amy's car was in its usual place. Jay and Amy had taken her car to Marietta, so they were back and, with no lights in her apartment, he knew she was fast asleep.

Davis was careful to make no noise so as not to awake his daughter next door as he entered his own apartment. *What a night! I thought once I moved back home to Adairsville life would be simple. Who would have guessed?* He quickly dressed for bed and crawled under the covers, but his mind could not get away from the events of the evening which deprived him of sleep for much of the night.

Deidre had only been in Albany a few days but she already missed Davis, especially this night. Usually Monday was her favorite day, because of her standing date for the weekly dinner with Davis and Amy. She loved the fact that Davis refused to let any distraction short of a serious emergency interrupt this tradition. The history teacher felt cheated because she was two hundred miles away in the South Georgia town of Albany on a night she normally spent with the people she enjoyed most.

Davis was probably home and had, by now, eaten alone. That bothered her more than it should. Amy, no doubt, would be with Jay. Adairsville had become home very quickly for her, even before she reached the halfway point of her first year in the classroom at Adairsville High. She missed it all, but she scolded herself when she realized she missed Davis most. If a serious relationship was to develop between the two of them, she wanted Davis to be the instigator. She was determined she would simply put it in the Lord's hands and honor his timing.

"You haven't said much tonight." The voice was that of Deidre's friend, Barbara Mason, a lady she had known and loved for a long time. "Is there something on your mind?"

"You know me," said Deidre. "There is always a lot on my mind. I think sometimes I spend so much time with my thoughts that I don't have time left to get very much done." *The Den Mother*, she repeated in her mind the nickname she and the other girls in the youth group secretly gave Barbara when the lady who missed absolutely nothing was the wife of their preacher. She was almost always responsible for them on church trips, and never failed to take her chaperon duties rather seriously. *Ten years ago, I doubt I would have agreed to let the Den mother be my roommate.*

"Is there someone special you miss back in Adairsville?" she questioned her soon-to-be roommate while putting some books in a box.

"Maybe ... no..., I don't think so..., but there could be...," Deidre mumbled, not really knowing how to respond to Barbara's question.

"Well, that is as clear as mud. I didn't mean to confuse you, honey. I was just making conversation."

"I'm sorry. It's just that the whole deal has me so perplexed. I guess I don't know where we stand or even if he has any real affection for me beyond friendship, but I like him a lot. I think I may even love him. It's just that there are so many complications. You will meet him soon because he is our landlord and Amy's father, and there is seventeen years' difference in our ages. He almost worshipped his wife who passed away less than two years ago, and I don't know if he will ever get over her enough to devote himself to anyone else. There, you have it all in a nutshell." Deidre was embarrassed almost to tears that she had opened her mouth to let the whole complicated ball of wax come flying out all at once.

"Well, obviously there are some areas of concern, but obstacles can be removed or climbed over. It sounds to me like the two of you need to sit down and talk if there is to be even a remote possibility of any serious romance."

"I know eventually that will have to happen, but I don't know that we are ready for that talk. When we are, I think Davis will take the lead to make it happen."

"I don't know, honey; if Davis is like most men, he may never show that kind of initiative. Communication is not their strong point. You may have to push him a little."

"Maybe you are right. It's true Davis can be rather private. He is not someone you would describe as an extrovert, but I can't fault him for that. I'm a little like that myself. However, he is the sort of person who will speak up when his heart dictates. I know he loves me as a friend, but I get the idea he is unsure if there is or should be anything beyond that. If or when he decides he loves me, I don't think he will hesitate to tell me." She continued to wrap and pack small breakables for the trip to North Georgia.

"I don't mean to complicate matters further, sweetheart, but I have to tell you that Ted is excited about seeing you." Barbara made reference to her second son who would arrive in Albany on Wednesday from Savannah to drive the U-Haul truck, packed with his mother's belongings, to Adairsville on Thursday. "I know the two of you were sweet on each other before he left for college. In fact, back then, I dreamed you would someday be my daughter-in-law.

Deidre was not surprised to hear Barbara's confession. "Ted and Mandy seemed happy though," Deidre said, "especially when they had their little boy."

"I know," Barbara said. "I can't believe it's been three years since the wreck."

"Losing a wife and baby son that way must have been awful for Ted," said Deidre. "How is he doing now?"

"He dates, but usually doesn't stay with any one girl very long. He just hasn't found the right one yet. I guess I had high hopes that would change when he got reacquainted with you."

So that is it, Deidre thought. *That is why she has been prodding me about whether there is someone special in Adairsville. She is still playing matchmaker.* "It will be good to see Ted again," she politely responded. "I called him after he lost Mandy and the baby, but we have had no contact since."

"Ted is a good boy with a lot of positive attributes. He just needs to decide what he wants out of life. He has done well in the banking business, highly regarded in that circle, but he doesn't seem to want to stay in one place very long. It seems like he has just about covered the banks in Savannah." Barbara pulled the flaps of the box she had packed with some of her favorite books down before securing it with packing tape.

"A friend who is a banker told me that is sort of the nature of the profession. Banks are prone to hire people who already have contacts in the community." Deidre tried her best to turn the conversation away from Barbara's attempt at matchmaking. It wasn't that she did not like Ted. She remembered him as a fantastic human being, but it was Davis who had taken possession of her heart, and right now that left very little room for anyone else. She just hoped he felt the same way.

The clock approached ten o'clock and she wondered where Davis was and what he was doing. *He is probably home bored out of his mind, getting ready to go to bed. This panic mood I am experiencing is probably just due to the current distance between us.* She did not fully convince herself, and she went to bed that night with the uncomfortable feeling that all was not exactly right back in Adairsville. She would call tomorrow morning to make sure there were no serious problems in her little world.

CHAPTER 2

J ay and Amy entered the Corra Harris Bookshop of which Davis, a longtime book lover, was proud to be founder, proprietor, and only employee. The couple to be married in less than two weeks meandered through several shops located in the 1902 Stock Exchange building in order to get to the bookshop. Davis looked up as they both entered beaming.

"We made our decision," Amy declared. "We talked about it last night during the storm and went to the realtor's office this morning to inform him. We will know the date of the closing before the day is over. We decided to buy the old Ammon place."

Jay, usually quieter and more reserved than his fiancée, could not hold back his excitement. He jumped into the conversation almost before Amy finished her sentence.

"It will mean a lot of work for us, but we love the idea of having a house in the country with big oak shade trees and the nearest neighbor is a quarter of a mile away. The Folsom community is the kind of quaint little area that we have dreamed about. It's just an old farmhouse, but it has great potential. My dad taught me enough about carpentry to enable me to do most of the work myself. Can you believe they accepted our offer of eighteen thousand dollars less than listed? That discount will enable us to restore it just the way it should be. And the beauty of it all," he continued, "is it comes with ten acres."

Davis was thrilled for the excitement he heard from his daughter and soon to be son-in-law.

"As long as you know what is ahead of you," Davis cautioned the young couple. "You know Amy will be back in the classroom soon. She will have little time to help. And Jay, you will be trapped in that office in Atlanta much of the time. They didn't transfer you from Florida to Atlanta to allow you to spend most of your time in Adairsville."

"Oh, Dad, we can handle it. We don't expect it to be a breeze, but how often have you told me that very few worthwhile projects come easy?" Amy put her arms around Davis's neck and pulled his face close to hers. "I'm all grown up, Dad. I even have plans to get married before the end of the month. You don't need to worry about me."

"I know I don't, but that doesn't mean I can't if I want to." Davis smiled at his only daughter then kissed her on the forehead. "You two do whatever you want to do. If that is the house you have decided to buy, then I am with you. I will help you any way I can short of becoming a sheetrock worker or painter. Did I hear you say the house comes with ten acres? I thought the Ammon place was a farm with a great deal more acreage than that."

"Yes, I understand it was once an almost two-hundred-acre farm, but only ten will be sold with the house," Jay informed him. "Ten is plenty for us. Some of it is in pasture which means Amy can, in time, have the horses she always wanted."

"That should keep her happy." Davis recalled when his daughter was a teenager, while he pastored the Grandview Church in Indianapolis Indiana, she often spent weekends with a friend outside the city near Shelbyville. She did so not only because she loved her friend's company, but also because she got to ride 'Ten Speed,' one of the family horses. Amy's voice brought the proud father back to the present.

"They tell me the house is over one hundred years old and no one has lived in it for almost four years, so you can imagine how run-down it is, but that just means it will be ours in every respect. We can restore it however we please." Amy, always the optimistic one, continued, "Most of the rooms are gigantic and there are three bedrooms, enough for you to have your own room when you want to get away from Adairsville to enjoy the country."

"I really do appreciate that," Davis told his daughter, "but I've got a pretty comfortable nest just across the railroad tracks that meet most all my needs." Davis gestured with his right arm as he pointed in the direction of the big white Victorian house his mother left to him. He lived in half of the old house while Amy and her roommate, Deidre Ross, lived in the apartment on the other side of the big hallway that ran through the middle of his childhood home. "You don't have to give me a room. I sleep best when I am in my own bed, but I would appreciate you keeping a place set for me at the table," he said, laughing.

Davis knew someday he would convert his mother's old place back to a one-family residence. It had occurred to him that the perfect time to do that would be immediately after Amy's wedding when she would move out to start her own home with Jay, but he could not bring himself to do it now. Davis was rather fond of Deidre and that affection grew day by day. It was a real bonus for him to have the personable twenty-nine-year-old history teacher next door. He readily agreed several weeks earlier that Deidre and a longtime friend of hers, Barbara Mason, would occupy the other apartment for the immediate future. Mrs. Mason, he was told, was recently widowed. With Deidre's recommendation she would move to Adairsville where she had been hired to teach at the high school.

"The next big step for us is to locate an apartment to live in while we bring the Ammon place up to snuff," said Jay, "and it is a step that needs to be taken rather quickly, like yesterday. Do you know of any place we could rent without the usual one-year lease?"

Jay, the engineer, was always the practical one, no doubt, more at ease when details were clearly mapped out. With only twelve days before they would be married and with no place in which to live tied down, Davis figured his future son-in-law was on the verge of panic.

"Right off the bat I don't know of any such place, but I will ask around. I'll give Charley a call. He seems to keep tabs on such matters around town."

"By the way, Dad, I heard that Charley, in the midst of that terrible storm last night, found a body. Do you know anything about that?"

After a moment of silence Davis reluctantly answered his daughter's question. "I know a little about it since I was with him when he found the corpse near the creek out on Woody Road."

"What do you mean you were with him? I would hope I do not have to remind you that you have better things to do than ride around in the worst storm of the summer in a police car. Charley can handle the drunks and the traffic violations on his own. As far as I know he is the policeman and you are the bookseller," Amy sarcastically added.

Davis understood that Amy was not sold on his partnership with the Adairsville Police Department. He had found her more than a bit protective of him, especially since she lost her mom. He recognized why both he and his daughter had a tendency to be more anxious about each other's activities than they should be. It was almost as if in the past they didn't worry too much because they knew Julie would keep every situation in check. Now that they didn't have Julie to watch their backs, they worried about each other.

"The situation with the body was not a matter to be concerned about. The man wasn't the victim of violence. He died of natural causes. His body was stolen from the funeral home sometime in the night and then dumped on the side of the road. It was probably nothing more than a prank. When I talked with Charley this morning, he told me the corpse was a man by the name of Juan Norris visiting Adairsville from Santa Barbara, Brazil. He died of a heart attack while at one of the motels."

"What was he doing in Adairsville? We don't get a lot of tourist from places like Brazil. There has got to be a story behind that," the always curious Amy remarked.

"We haven't figured that out yet, but we will," Davis answered with a tone of confidence.

"I don't want to hear you talk about 'we.'" Amy told her father. "Remember, you are not a cop. We will all be better off if you remember that."

"What do you hear from Deidre?" Davis asked in an attempt to change the subject. "I would think a week would be long enough for anyone to swat mosquitoes in South Georgia," he said, laughing. "I told her I could come to Albany to drive the U-Haul to Adairsville if she needed me."

"Maybe that wouldn't be a bad idea," Amy suggested. "A trip to South Georgia might keep you out of patrol cars and away from dead bodies. I got a call from her earlier today. Her first question was about you. I told her you were fine, but at the time I didn't know you were out in the storm last night uncovering corpses. I think Mrs. Mason's son, Ted, is coming to drive the U-Haul.

"It was good of her to make the trip South to help Mrs. Mason pack and load for the move, but that is the kind of person Deidre is," Davis remarked to his daughter. "Friends like your roommate are hard to find."

"You don't have to sell me on Deidre; I've never had a better friend. She is the big sister I always wanted."

Jay, who for a time sat and listened patiently, finally got up from his position in one of the chairs Davis had placed in the shop. "We have got to go if we are to make it to Folsom and then back to town in time for our final premarital session with Pastor John." He was already walking toward the front door which he opened, raising his eyebrows at his fiancée.

"Remember what I said!" Amy called back to her dad, "No more corpses and no more police cars. Stick to your Bible and your books and you are much more likely to enjoy a long life."

"I hear you," Davis assured her with a grin on his face.

The middle-aged man used his handkerchief to mop the sweat from his forehead even though the air was running full blast in his late model Buick. It was his arranged meeting with those two rather unsavory characters that had him a little uneasy. He was never comfortable around such low-class specimens as those two, but as much as he disliked them, he was going to need the kind of help they could provide. He wanted someone who was willing to step outside the law and keep quiet. He knew that going outside the law would be no problem for them, but he worried about them keeping quiet.

It was their lack of intellectual capacity that bothered him most. He highly valued brain power and, in that department, the tall one and the wide one came up sadly lacking. Maybe he could keep them on track with a little micromanagement along with a lot of monetary motivation.

He was glad they had agreed to meet him in an isolated wooded area. The last thing he wanted was for anyone to see him anywhere near these two jailbirds. *They will have to do,* he decided. *This kind of work is outside my comfort zone. I could really have used them at that funeral home. Let them get their hands dirty. I'll keep mine clean.*

He saw the white Ford pickup and knew he was in the right place. There they were in front of the truck, *as odd a pair as you could ever imagine,* he thought. *It is hard for me to believe I'm stooping this low.*

It was late in the day and Davis's mind turned toward dinner. He would close in a few minutes and though he was mildly hungry, he didn't want to again go alone to a restaurant. He decided he would call Charley to see if he would join him at one of the local eateries.

Davis took his cell out of his pocket and punched his friend's number. Davis heard Charley's voice, "Hello, Charley Nelson speaking."

"Do you have plans for dinner, Charley? Since I'm not in the mood to eat alone, I will buy someone a free meal at a restaurant of their choice. Are you interested?"

The young man's response came from his lighthearted side that often showed itself when he was in a good mood. "Ordinarily I would jump at an offer like that, even if it meant I had to spend the evening with a boring old preacher-bookseller, but not tonight. I have a date with Cindy, and choosing between you and a tall beautiful blond who adores me is no contest."

"No, I guess there is no chance I can win that one. You behave yourself and try to get home at a reasonable hour. You need your rest."

Charley laughed before he responded, "Are you my mom or what—did you ever know me to stay out late? Enjoy yourself and be sure to drink some warm milk before you go to bed, I hear that is good for old geezers," he teased Davis before he abruptly left the line.

Davis's prayer life had sadly become almost nonexistent in the months of spiritual struggle after Julie's death, but now the exercise was once again vital to him. The former pastor bowed his head to silently pray for his friend. *Lord, help me to know what I can do to point Charley your way. Watch over him tonight. Guard his actions. Give him a conscience that will keep him in your will at all times. Help him to come to the knowledge that you love him and want what's best for him.*

Davis closed the shop and drove to the nearby Food Lion to search for his dinner. He was never much of a hand in the kitchen, but surely there would be some kind of delicacy he could purchase that wouldn't be too much trouble to prepare, yet would satisfy his need for a real meal. On the ride to the grocery store his mind, as it so often did these days, turned to Deidre. He wished she was home. He had found that lonesomeness was pretty much a way of life since his beloved Julie had been taken from him. It seemed to be worse at meals and during the quietness of the nights than any other time. His love for her had not dimmed, and he desperately missed her companionship. With just a little bit of guilt, Davis looked forward to day after tomorrow.

CHAPTER 3

"It's Jessica Fletcher," Red Edwards, owner of the Adairsville hardware store, pointed toward Davis when he walked into the crowded Little Rock Café. Each of the other three men seated around the big table with Red chuckled at his attempt at humor. The breakfast group of longtime friends in addition to Red included banker Al Jensen, Charley's brother Dean Nelson who operated an automobile garage in his home town, and Fire Chief Brad Dewelt. Davis often had breakfast with this crowd, though he sometimes wondered why he put himself through such torture. All of them seemed to take great delight in giving him a hard time, but then they really didn't single him out. None of the group was exempt from their good-natured, but sometimes cruel, bantering. Davis knew the reference to Jessica Fletcher was in regards to the New England writer in the old TV mystery series that seemed to turn up a corpse everywhere she went.

Davis sat down in one of the two unoccupied chairs at the table. "Isn't anything sacred to you, guys? That man was a human person who was probably someone's father. Don't you heathens have any respect for the dead?"

Brad took up the lighthearted discussion. "Sure we do, but none of us has ever found a body. How many are you up to now? You hold some kind of record, don't you? It's scary just to be around you. Who knows, one of us could end up as one of your corpses."

"It wouldn't be so bad if you didn't always drag my little brother into your messes," Dean accusingly directed his remarks toward his friend who had lined up next to him at Tiger stadium for two full seasons. Davis was the guy who caught the football while Dean was the one who protected the quarterback long enough to get the ball to the sure-handed receiver.

"You have it all wrong," Davis informed him. "Charley found the body. I just happened to be along for the ride."

"That may be true," Brad replied, "but you are the body magnet. If he had not been with you, he probably never would have come across that poor man. What can I say? You draw dead people like slop draws flies."

Davis was glad when Brenda, the waitress who always managed to wait on their table, made her way over to them and inquired, "Do you down-and-out gentlemen expect a handout or do you want me to take your order today?" They all gave the waitress their order, though they really didn't need to. She had long ago committed to memory what each man ordered each day. "Not that any of you are in a rut," she told them.

The young lady, dressed in the blue uniform-of-the-day, gracefully moved away from their table. Al remarked, "Brenda seems to be on her best behavior. Maybe that means we can expect better service today."

"I think it means she didn't get enough sleep last night and is too tired to make our lives miserable this morning." Red laughed when the waitress turned around to stick her tongue out at them.

"Incidentally, guys, do any of you know of any decent apartments available in town that would not require the traditional one-year lease? Jay and Amy will tie the knot in less than a week and a half but haven't yet found a place to live. They are buying the old Ammon farm out near Folsom, but it will be a while before they get it ready for occupancy."

"Did you say the Ammon place?" Red sounded surprised. "Surely you don't mean the Ammon farm? Why, that old place is in terrible condition and besides, I've heard for years that it is haunted. I never believed it before, but maybe there is something to it. I passed there on a recent Saturday night after eleven o'clock. I could see a light in the front of the house. I figured it had to be ghosts since no one has lived there in years."

"Isn't that where the bones were found in the cave about a hundred years ago?" Dean asked. "Maybe you saw the people who once occupied those skeletons," he said, laughing.

"I think you're right," Brad responded. "Bones were found there. I've heard that not much was made of it at the time because it was during World War I when the public was only concerned about what was happening in Europe. If I remember correctly, the cave was sealed years ago. And that's too bad," he added. "Do you remember those cave spelunking adventures we took in our teen years? You went with us on a couple of those underground excursions didn't you, Davis?"

"Yes, I did, but if my memory serves me correctly, it was more like four or five trips. I've been trying to forget them for the last thirty years. With no equipment and no common sense, it is a wonder any of us survived. Did anyone ever figure out where the bones found in the Ammon cave came from?" Davis asked.

"Not to my knowledge," Brad answered. "I've heard everything from it being an ancient Indian burial ground to the site of a mass murder. Who knows?"

"Davis. I think I can help Jay and Amy," Al spoke up. "The bank has several repossessed properties we would like to rent. None of them are in perfect condition, but a couple of them would be suitable temporarily. Have Jay and Amy come by the bank sometime today or tomorrow if they are interested. We can at least talk about it. I think I can fix them up with a good deal."

"Thanks, Al, I'll relay the message later today. Sounds like it could be the perfect solution for their problem."

"You just want to be sure they don't move in with you," Brad accused the soon-to-be father of the bride.

"I don't think there is any danger of that," Davis told him before he took a bite of the scrambled eggs placed in front of him only moments before. "I don't think Jay is interested in that much time with his father-in-law."

The good-humored bantering continued around the table until each man finished his meal and left for his respective place of business.

As was his custom, Davis dropped by the post office before he went to the bookshop. He was thrilled to find a small package in his box. He immediately removed the tape from the package to find exactly what he had hoped for—the first edition copy of *To Kill a Mocking Bird* he had found online. He looked closely at the copyright page to make sure it was indeed what he ordered. It was all there. The printed information showed it was published by Lippincott in 1960 with first edition stated and no mention of any other editions. It was indeed one of the original 5,000 copies. Davis was excited to hold such a rare and sought-after book in his hand. It was without dust jacket, but he would soon remedy that.

Davis greeted Janie, the personable 1902 Stock Exchange clerk when he came through the front door. "Expecting a big day, Janie?"

"Oh, they are all about the same," she told him. "We do have a couple of bus tours booked for lunch at the tea room around noon. Maybe they will buy some books."

"I hope so. I've got to pay for a wedding as well as a new Jeep. I need to unload some serious stock."

The bookseller with his package under his arm proceeded toward one of the back corners where the Corra Harris Bookshop was the chief attraction. Preoccupied with the package in his hands, he at first did not hear the familiar voice behind him.

"Wait up, Dad." It was Amy who entered the store, walking at a faster-than-normal pace to catch up to her father who at six-foot tall had legs considerably longer than those connected to her five-foot-six frame. "Why are you in such a hurry?"

"I've got this special package that I can't wait to marry up with its partner back here in the desk drawer." He pulled the book he had just received out of its package and proudly held it up for his daughter to see.

"It's just an old book with no dust jacket," she observed.

"Look at the title." Davis turned the book to allow Amy to see its spine. "It is a first edition of *To Kill a Mocking Bird*," the bookseller explained to his daughter. "I have here a library copy of the same book. Of course it has library markings and it is rather ragged so it has only minimal value, but when I take the true first edition dust jacket off the retired library copy, take it out of its protective cover and remove the label from the bottom of the spine and then place that dust jacket on this book which is also a true first edition...," he pointed toward the copy he had just taken out of the package, "I will have a book worth between ten and fifteen thousand dollars. I paid a little more than one thousand dollars for the two volumes, but they should provide for me at least a month's wages. I'll keep it in the locked display case to show off for a while, but when funds get really low I will likely sell it online."

"Wow, that's great, Dad!" Amy declared. "That will pay for my wedding!"

"Maybe, but we probably shouldn't count the money until it is sold, though that shouldn't be a problem since it is currently the most sought-after collectable published in America. I have often heard it called the great American novel."

"Well. I'm happy for you, Dad, and I also have good news: we will close on the house next Thursday."

"Fantastic!" her father sincerely responded. "Two days before the big day. When will you take possession?"

"That will happen immediately after we close. We can leave the lawyer's office to go straight to the house to start work on the new roof if we decide that is what we want to do. We almost lost it though," Amy added. "A Mr. Johnson from out of town yesterday afternoon offered the full price, and the owners almost took it. And who could have blamed them if they had done so, but they graciously decided that even though we had not yet signed the contract, the ethical thing to do was to let us have it at the agreed price."

"That speaks well of them. I hope you told them that."

"I gave both of them a big hug and expressed my undying appreciation. I assured them they will be among our special friends forever, and I meant it."

"I think we can add one other item to the current rejoice list," her father told her. "Al Jenson told me to have you and Jay drop by to see him sometime today or tomorrow. The bank has some properties available to rent that he feels might meet your needs until you get the house ready."

"Great! I was about to panic over where we would live for the next six months or so. I'll go get Jay when I leave here. I know he is just as anxious to tie that little detail down as I am. Time is certainly getting short." Amy hugged her dad before she left. "I love you, Dad. Thank you for all you have done for me and Jay."

Later in the day Charley showed up in uniform at the Corra Harris Bookshop still hobbling from his unexpected trip down the bank the night of the storm. "Have you found homes for any of those smelly old books today?" he spoke to Davis who had his back turned to him to stand on a short stepladder with a duster in his hand.

"Only a couple," the bookseller responded; "and those two transactions won't even buy my dinner tonight. "What can I show you? Here is one you might be interested in." He pointed at the copy of *To Kill a Mockingbird* he had only an hour earlier placed in the glass showcase and carefully placed a card atop the cover which stated the price to be $12,500.00. "It's a real bargain," he told his friend who had little appreciation for collectable books.

"You've got to be kidding," Charley said, sounding shocked. "There is no book in existence worth that much money."

"I know there is nothing I can say to convince you, but that one is worth that much and perhaps more. You just wait! I'll sell it for the stated price in less than three months. I tell you what ... we will make a wager. If I sell it for that amount or more in the next three months you buy me dinner, but if I don't, I'll buy you the biggest steak to be found in three counties."

"You've got yourself a deal," Charley told him. "I came by to give you a report on our tattooed man. You might keep it all under your hat. The chief didn't tell me it was confidential, but I guess he assumed I knew that. So if you go blab what I tell you all over town, I will probably be in big trouble."

"I appreciate any information you can give me, and I promise it will not go any further than right here."

"Okay—in that case, I can tell you that two people at the Cracker Barrel recalled that Mr. Norris ate dinner there a couple of times. They remembered him by the tattoos that covered both arms and even showed above his shirt collar. Charlotte, one of the waitresses, told me there was a middle-aged man with him on one of his visits. That man was around six-foot tall, hair thin, and she remembered that he was rather well-dressed. She thought the tattooed man referred to the other man as Reed, but she said she could be wrong since his accent made it difficult to understand. I asked the girl at the motel desk if there was anyone by the name of Reed who stayed there at the same time as Juan Norris. She at first said she didn't know if she could ethically reveal that information without permission, but I am sure it was because she found me so attractive that she finally came around to tell me there was no *Reed* registered while Norris was there. I also told her I would like to have her phone number."

"You never stop, do you?" Davis scolded his friend. "You can't turn off your Romeo impersonation even long enough to be a cop. Did you really say that?"

Charley only smiled when he opened the file folder he held in his hand. "Take a look at this picture of the dead man's chest and stomach. Can you make any sense out of these symbols tattooed across his chest and upper stomach? I thought it looked like Latin or maybe Greek."

"No. I had Latin in high school and spent a great deal of time with Greek back in my seminary days, and I can assure you this is neither. Some of the symbols are similar to those found in both those alphabets, but this isn't Greek or Latin. It's possible I might be able to help you with this if you can leave the picture with me," Davis suggested.

"I enlarged two copies, so you can keep that one. There is one more item. One of the attendants out at the QT station remembered a tattooed man came in to ask about the location of a cave out that way, perhaps several miles east of there. The clerk told him he could not help him since he had never heard of such a cave anywhere near there."

Davis's ears perked up a little when he received that last bit of information. *So the tattooed man from Brazil by the name of Juan Norris attempted to locate a particular cave in the Adairsville area?* Interesting," he said more to himself than to Charley.

"Incidentally, there were reports that a late model gray Buick Encore was seen in the lot behind the funeral home the night the body was stolen. Well, I've got to go. I've got a lot to do. The chief can get mighty disagreeable when I show up late. Keep me informed about what you learn about those tattooed symbols." Charley hurried toward the front door, but did not walk through it until he stopped for a moment to flirt with Janie who only laughed at his Don Juan impersonation.

It was a busy time for Amy. Wedding preparation was fun, but it required a lot of work. When she finally got a few minutes to sit down, her thoughts went to her dad. Until now, she had given only token consideration to where her marriage to Jay left him. *He had a wonderful life with Mom, but that part of his life is over. I have Jay, but he has no one.*

In recent weeks Amy had observed that her father's interest in her twenty-nine-year-old roommate went well beyond the fondness that a father might ordinarily have for his daughter's best friend. That pleased her despite the seventeen or eighteen years' difference in their ages. *Dad needs someone,* she reasoned, *and so does Deidre. Why should a few years' difference in age matter? They are perfect for one another. I only wish there was some action I could take to encourage them to see that. Well, there is one—I can pray....*

CHAPTER 4

Davis awakened on Thursday morning with the sun shining through his raised bedroom window. Birds chirped from the trees in his yard and, best of all, Deidre would be home later in the day. *Life is good,* he decided.

Davis was often up before daylight not because it was necessary, but because he, more often than not, found himself involuntarily wide awake in those early hours, but this morning he actually slept until almost eight o'clock. He showered, dressed, and prepared a quick breakfast of oatmeal, orange juice, and coffee. He needed to hurry because he had told Jay he would arrive at his motel no later than nine o'clock. One of Davis's pet peeves was irresponsible people who were always late. He needed to secure the permanent license plate for his new Jeep while Jay had a fine to pay for a rolling stop. Both items of business would need to be handled in Cartersville, the Bartow county seat, so the two men decided they might as well make the trip together.

The Jeep pulled into the motel space at five minutes till the hour. Davis parked the vehicle and strode to the door marked with a big "eight." Davis knocked before he called out.

"Jay, I'm here!" He then backed away, an instinctive move left over from his days in the ministry. Proper ministerial procedure for house visits called for one to move away from the door after he knocked or rang the doorbell.

There was noise inside the room that sounded as if someone had bumped against a piece of furniture, but still after three or four minutes Jay did not come to the door. Finally, Davis took the four steps needed to return to where he could again knock, this time a little more vigorously than before. "Jay, you in there?" Davis called loud enough for his future son-in-law to hear even behind the closed door. He heard a noise similar to the one he heard before.

"Davis! I'm in trouble! Call the police!" Again there was a bumping and scrambling sound from inside the room. Davis backed away to pull his cell from his pocket just as the door flew open. A tall lean man with a gun in his hand stood in front of him.

"Put away the phone!" the man demanded before he looked to the right and then to the left, no doubt to see if he and his gun had been spotted. When he was satisfied no one could see him, he motioned with his gun hand and sneered at Davis, "Get in here right now or I'll drop you where you stand." Fear rushed through Davis's whole body. Julie had always hated guns. Her fear of them had long ago rubbed off on her husband.

Davis mustered enough courage to gently speak. "Brother, I wish you would point that gun in another direction. It might go off." For obvious reason, the name "Stringbean" came to Davis's mind as he stared at the seemingly undernourished character in front of him.

"I'll point this gun in any direction I choose. You are dead right—it could go off at any moment, so you had better do as I say."

While he held to the gun with his right hand, he closed the door with his left after Davis walked forward through the entrance. It was then that Davis realized there was another thug in the room. The features of this one were just the opposite of those of Stringbean. This stranger who held Jay's arm behind his back was close to a foot and a half shorter than his partner, and he was very, very wide. Davis immediately thought of a sumo wrestler. He took note that this man also had a gun.

His weapon was tucked under his belt. Davis was able to see it when his unbuttoned jacket opened wide enough for it to become partially visible.

The sumo wrestler spoke with a slight accent Davis could not put his finger on.

"We don't really want to hurt anyone," he explained with a smirk. "Our job here is to deliver a message, but you had better understand it is an important message. To ignore what we're going to tell you could be dangerous or even fatal. Listen closely," he said distinctly. He continued to hold Jay's arm behind his back. "You really don't want that farm east of here. I think it's sometimes called the Ammon farm. It would not be healthy for you or that pretty bride of yours to sign any of those papers. We are here only because we are worried about you," he added.

Davis, whose face became flushed at the sumo wrestler's threat, jumped in to offer a warning of his own. "Mister, I don't know who you are or what this is about, but that is my daughter you are talking about. You be assured that if you lay a finger on her I will leave no stone unturned to find you, and if I can't get the job done, there are others who care about her who will—and some of those people are law enforcement officers." Davis's anger was triggered by the reference to Amy, and brought out a boldness not typical of him.

"You do what you are told and there will be no problems for any of us. If this boy signs those papers or if any money changes hands...," "Sumo" paused and glanced toward Jay, "it will open a nasty can of worms. We don't play games. I could shoot both of you right now which would take care of our problem, and I will if it comes to that. There are plenty of houses for sale. You'll not have to look hard to find one better than that old shack in the middle of nowhere. You don't want to mess up your future."

"We will leave you now, but I hope you will remember what my partner told you." It was Stringbean who said his good byes while he backed toward the door with gun still in hand. "It would not be a good idea for you to tell anyone about our little visit, and that includes the law."

"I hope we won't have to get together again," "Sumo" added with a twisted smile when he released his hold on Jay's arm and joined his pal to leave the room. Even in the seriousness of the moment, Davis could not help but think of the old Laurel and Hardy movies. The tall skinny guy and his short heavy partner disappeared when they closed the door behind them.

After a moment had gone by, Davis darted to the window to pull the curtains back to see if he could get a glimpse of the intruder's car or maybe even get a license plate number, but evidently the two tough guys had disappeared around the corner. Davis immediately jerked open the door to hurry outside, but again saw nothing. When he returned to the room, Jay sat on the bed with his face in his hands.

"Are you okay?" Davis questioned Jay. "Do I need to take you to the hospital to be checked out?"

"No, they didn't hurt me. Why all this trouble about an old farmhouse?" Jay looked up at his future father-in-law with fear, or perhaps it was frustration in his eyes. "All we want to do is find a decent place to start our lives together. Why would anyone object to our buying that property? It has been up for sale for months without as much as a nibble."

"I don't know. Didn't you or Amy tell me that someone made an offer in the last day or two?"

"Yes, I think it was a Mr. Johnson from some place out of town. Do you think he was behind this? Maybe one of those men was Johnson," Jay speculated.

"Maybe so; I don't know, but I do know we need to get to the police station to report this."

"Do you think we should do that in light of the warning we were given? It might really set them off."

"I don't care what they said; we need to report what happened here to the police. You have Amy to consider."

Davis and Jay found Chief Hanson at the station. They took about twenty minutes of his time to tell him their story. Davis provided a description of the two villains. Though he didn't seem very concerned, the chief assured them that his officers would be on the lookout for the thugs and suggested to Jay that he and Amy needed to have someone with them at all times.

On the way to Cartersville, Jay and Davis made some plans. "I assume you will not let those hoods scare you away. Are you sure you want to go through with the purchase?"

"Yes," Jay responded, "Absolutely. That is the house Amy wants and that is the one she will have. I will not let a little abuse from a couple of Laurel and Hardy look-alikes scare me away." Jay seemed somewhat less frightened now that the initial attack on him was more than an hour removed.

The decision was made by the two men that Jay would immediately move into the little yellow house on College Street that Al had rented to them. A couple of friends he had met through Amy could be recruited to help him move some of her things to that location on Saturday. It would be safer for him there since the house is only a stone's throw away from the Police Department building. That move would also free up some space for Mrs. Mason. Amy could remain in the apartment with Deidre and Barbara until the wedding or she could make use of her dad's spare bedroom, which ever she decided on. "We need to let Amy know of the threats, but let's not tell her more than we have to," Davis suggested. "There is no reason to tell her those guys got rough with you or that they had guns. But we do need to keep our eyes on her at all times."

"That's not hard for me," Jay admitted with a laugh. "I've had a hard time keeping my eyes off her ever since we met in our first year of college."

Later in the day Davis remembered the photo of the tattoos which Charley had passed on to him. He sat down at his computer to see if his initial suspicions were correct. He googled "Cherokee Alphabet" which enabled him to bring up an image of the complete alphabet put together by a Native American by the name of Sequoyah around 1800. Davis discovered that his first impression was correct. The markings on the chest and upper stomach of the deceased tattooed man were indeed images from the Cherokee alphabet. *Why would a Brazilian national have a portion of the Cherokee alphabet tattooed on his body? What are the chances of that happening? Yet....*

The curious bookman continued to read from the website on the screen to find a number of interesting facts about the Cherokees and their native language. Charley had the day off; Davis decided to call the policeman to report what he had discovered. "Charley, this is Davis; I hope your day has been better than mine."

"Yeah—you can't stay out of trouble, can you? I stopped by the station earlier and the chief told me about your problem this morning. He said you told him some story about threats from Stringbean and Sumo Wrestler. The last time you got into trouble like this it was the Rat-Faced Man. Don't you ever meet any bad guys that look normal?"

"I guess I just tend to draw the really ugly element. Apparently these cutthroats do not want Jay and Amy to take possession of the Ammon farm, and they used guns to make their point. But let me tell you why I called. I have some information about the tattoos on our dead man's chest and stomach. I am fairly certain those images are from the Cherokee alphabet."

"Don't kid me; why would a Brazilian man have the Cherokee Alphabet tattooed on his body?"

"It sounds a little strange to me too, but I am sure that is what it is. Those signs on his upper body are part of Sequoyah's Cherokee syllabary; eighty-five characters, and some of them, as you noted the other day, are similar to Greek and Latin letters."

"I cannot imagine how, but I guess that could be helpful information. The obvious question is—what do those syllables say?" the always inquisitive Charley questioned his friend.

"That's a good question. I found enough information online to equip an intelligent person to translate the symbols on the body of our corpse, but I'm talking about you and me. Maybe we had better get some expert help. I have a friend at Reinhardt University who is a

Cherokee scholar. With his help we should know in a matter of minutes if the tattoos on Mr. Norris's stomach have any significance to the case."

"Why don't you give your scholar friend a call to see if we can come out there Saturday before I have to go back to directing traffic and issuing tickets."

"I'll do that, but let me suggest we make one other stop before we see him. Would you go with me to see Jay and Amy's realtor? A man by the name of Johnson made an offer after theirs was accepted. I don't know if he has anything to do with the threats made by Stringbean and Sumo, but it is certainly worth considering. Maybe we can group the two visits tomorrow afternoon if it works for you."

"It sounds like a plan for a Saturday afternoon. You set up appointments with both people and I'll tag along." True to Charley's past pattern, there was no goodbye, see-you-later, or any clue the call would come to an end before there was only dead air on the line.

Any time now! Davis thought as he put his telephone back into his pocket. *Deidre and her crew should arrive at any time.* Another hour passed and still another without any sign of Mrs. Mason's U-Haul. Davis started to worry.

CHAPTER 5

Amy's voice brought Davis out of his stupor. His daughter came into the living room from the hallway which divided their apartments where he had been stationed all evening in his favorite chair to await the arrival of the crew from South Georgia.

"Dad, there has been an accident." Noticing that Davis's face immediately turned white, she quickly gave a word of assurance. "No one was hurt!" She explained, "Deidre just called to tell us that when they got off the interstate to get gas, there was a collision with a driver who was apparently drunk."

Color gradually came back to Davis's face when he heard that no one was injured. "What happened? Were both the truck and Mrs. Mason's car involved in the accident?"

"No, Deidre said the drunk driver ran a red light which caused the truck in which she and Ted were in to plow into the back side of his car. Barbara was at the wheel of her own car behind them, but luckily was far enough from the rear of the truck to stop before she crashed into it. Deidre and Ted came out without even a scratch. The driver of the car had some minor injuries, but evidently did not require hospitalization. Of course Ted was driving and Deidre gave him high marks for his ability and reflexes."

"I think I'll call Deidre." Davis had already pulled his phone out of his pocket to punch the speed dial number for Deidre even before he got the words out of his mouth.

Amy smiled; maybe it was her desire to give her father and her best friend some privacy that caused her to walk out of the living room into her dad's kitchen where she made her way over to the sink to find a couple of dishes which she proceeded to wash. Back in the other room, Davis was already on his phone with Deidre.

"I needed to make sure you are all right," Davis explained. "Amy gave me your report, but I needed to hear it from you. Are you sure you have no hidden injuries that will show up later? That happens, you know."

"I know it does, but no, Davis, I'm fine. We weren't traveling very fast, and since I could see the whole incident unfolding in front of me, I had time to brace myself. I may end up with a little soreness from the seatbelt and air bags doing their jobs, but I'm sure there is no real problem. I'm glad Ted was at the wheel. He handled what could have been a disastrous situation with a lot of skill and composure. Had he not swerved to avoid crashing straight into the driver's seat, the man in the car could very well have been killed. I will be grateful to him forever."

Davis was also thankful for the skill and quick reflexes of this man whom he had never met, and he tried his best, without complete success, not to feel jealous when Deidre spoke of gratefulness that would extent to forever. "So how does this affect your plans? When do you think you will get back to Adairsville?"

"I hope we will be able to get it all pulled together in the morning or at least by early afternoon. We will have to pick up another rental truck and transfer all Barbara's possessions from the wrecked one. Luckily all the damage is to the front of the truck. None of her belongings seem to be worse for wear. My guess is we will be able to make it home before dark tomorrow. We should be fine here at the motel tonight."

"Call me if you need me. You don't know how relieved I am that you are okay. I surely have missed you, and I can hardly wait for you to get back next door where I can keep close tabs on you." Davis said his goodbye and immediately wished he had not made that last statement. It sounded so possessive, perhaps as if he didn't trust her. He bowed his head to silently thank the Lord for her safety and that of her traveling companions. There was also a prayer for protection for the remainder of their trip.

Watch over them, Lord. Bring Deidre and her friends home to us. Guard them against every possible danger. Psalm 62:1–2, one of Davis's favorite passages of scriptures, came to his mind: *My soul finds rest in God alone; my salvation comes from him. He alone is my rock and my salvation; he is my fortress; I will never be shaken.*

Deidre continued to sit quietly in reflection for a few moments after Davis was no longer on the phone. There was a sense of satisfaction—or was it relief that came to her as a result of Davis's call? He cared enough to immediately make contact with her when he got the news of their troubles. *I don't know why I ever doubted he would. I know he cares. Thoughtfulness is second nature to him.* She knew it was time for her to join Barbara and Ted at the restaurant, but she took time to wash her hands and face and take her hair out of the ponytail to allow it to hang freely about her shoulders before she changed from the T-shirt and jeans she wore into an outfit a little more appropriate for dinner.

Ted and Barbara were already in seats at a table when she arrived.

"Over here," Barbara called and waved to her with that same uninhibited exuberance Deidre recalled from her youthful years when Barbara was so much a part of her life. There was a time when she dreamed she would someday be Mrs. Ted Mason. *Look at him sitting there with those tan blond surfer-boy good looks.* Since she had not been around Ted for years, she had forgotten until yesterday how charming he could be, yet there seemed to be a part of his former demeanor that was now missing. She wasn't sure what it was, but she knew he wasn't exactly the same as she remembered him. *Oh, well, we all change,* she reasoned. There was an empty chair between Ted and his mother. *Barbara, no doubt, was responsible for that,* she decided.

Since the three of them had come together on the previous day, they had often reminisced about days gone by, about joys almost forgotten, and about opportunities lost. Tonight was no exception.

"Do you remember going with me to the senior prom when I was a senior and you a junior?" Ted asked Deidre who was not so anxious to dwell on such memories.

"How could I forget it?" she answered; "It was the highlight of my life up to that time. How many shy awkward junior girls get to go to the prom with the handsome senior quarterback? I figured you had long since forgotten about that," Deidre added.

"Forgotten? I remember every detail of that wonderful evening. The way you looked in that beautiful yellow gown made just about every other guy there wish you were his date. Why, every time one of the other guys danced or even talked with you, I just about died of jealousy. It was one of those special occasions from high school that I couldn't forget if I tried. We had a lot of those days back then, but life seems to have gone downhill considerably since," Ted mused.

He's got so much going for him but he seems so unhappy, Deidre silently speculated. *I wonder if he still struggles with the loss of his wife and child after all these years., I know it is possible to hang on to grief forever, but I remember Ted being extremely tuned in to the spiritual side of life. I never thought him to be the kind to mope for the rest of his life.*

After dinner the trio strolled the short distance back to the motel.

"It has been a hard day and I am tired." Barbara stretched and yawned as she spoke. "I don't know about you, young people, but this old lady needs to hit the sack. Deidre, don't feel as if you have to go back to the room to keep me company. Feel free to use my car if there is somewhere the two of you would like to go."

"What about it, Deidre?" Ted turned toward Deidre who was beside him. "Would you like to see if we could find some kind of entertainment? We can pretend we are teenagers again out on the town."

"I appreciate the invitation, Ted, but I don't think so. The fact is I am not a teenager anymore, and I too am a bit tired. I think I'll go back to the room and read a while before I go to bed. I've just gotten started on the latest Terri Blackstock thriller and would like to get back to it. I read for relaxation, and I need to relax. Maybe we can go out on the town another time."

Ted used the remote to turn on the power to the TV in his room; then he punched numbers to look for a diversion that might help drown out the pain of another night alone. Loneliness had been a factor in his life for a long time, even before Mandy and Jerry were killed by that drunk driver three years ago. *Maybe that is just life,* he thought. *Maybe everyone walks around lonely or unhappy while they pretend otherwise. I know that is what I have done for the past ten years. Seeing Deidre has made it worse, because she reminds me of a time when I felt differently. It has actually become hard to remember when I enjoyed life and maybe that is best. You don't long so much for what you think you never had.*

He lay down the remote when he decided to watch the last couple of innings of the game between the Atlanta Braves and Washington Nationals. He half listened when Braves announcer Joe Simpson remarked, "For the first time in several days, Braves fans have something to be happy about. They have come back to take a big lead in this one."

"I wish it was that easy" Ted told himself in a voice barely loud enough to be heard. "I wish it was that easy." The TV was still on, but the game was over an hour later when he fell asleep.

Barbara Mason did come back to the room she and Deidre shared and immediately went to bed, but she had not yet managed to get to sleep. *It is one of those times,* she told herself, *one can get so tired and keyed up that it becomes hard to even sleep.* Deidre in the other bed read by the lamp on the nightstand beside her bed. Oh, how Barbara hoped and prayed that the youthful relationship Deidre and Ted once had would be reignited. *How has it been possible for a young lady with such a rare combination of beauty, brains, and common sense to reach twenty-nine years of age without matrimony. Ted is so unhappy and there is no doubt in my mind that Deidre could change that. I think Ted is interested, but it takes two to tango. Oh, well, we'll just have to put it in the Lord's hands; however, I don't think He will mind if I push it along. That is what mothers do, I suppose.* Barbara stayed very still in her bed so as not to cause Deidre to think the light from her lamp was responsible for her inability to sleep, but it was not until much later after Deidre turned off the light that Barbara finally fell asleep.

CHAPTER 6

Most of Davis's energy was used in his bookshop on Friday. During the middle of the afternoon, Amy received a call from Deidre who told her that they had just then picked up keys to a truck to make the remainder of the trip. By the time they loaded the truck it would be night time. Davis sighed when he learned it would be Saturday before they would arrive in Adairsville.

When Saturday morning came with all its promise, Davis was in a much better mood. To stroll down the street of the little town Davis called home almost always caused him to feel grateful for the opportunity to live in such a wonderful place as was this little "Norman Rockwell" community. Today was no exception. From time to time Davis liked to make contact with other merchants on the street, sometimes called the square, even though there was nothing square about it. On this bright morning he would say hello to Carol at The General Mercantile before he took care of a few duties at his own place of business. Perhaps he would even have a cup of the best tea in town served from her unique shop before he would face the work that was waiting on him.

Davis went past city hall, actually three buildings that had been gutted and remodeled to provide adequate space for the progressive small town to take care of its business. Mayor Sam Ellison got out of his car after he parked in a space in front of the marble-covered front that was once the bank but now housed the office of the town's chief executive. Seeing Davis, he grinned and waved.

"Out on this beautiful day to survey your kingdom, Mr. Mayor?" Davis inquired of the middle-aged mayor. "I thought city hall was closed on Saturdays."

"It is. I need to be home taking care of my lawn," the mayor answered. "But there is always city business to draw me down here even on days off. Incidentally," the mayor asked, "how are you coming with the book?"

Sam's reference to "the book" made Davis a little uneasy because he as yet had done very little work on the proposed history of Adairsville. The mayor and his cohorts commissioned Davis several weeks back to put it together. City officials had the idea that because he once authored a short inspirational book, and currently did a weekly newspaper column about growing up in Adairsville, he could write. Davis convinced the town bigwigs who had approached him that the best approach to take was not a true history, but rather a compilation of material about Adairsville that could, no doubt, be dug out by anyone who would take the time to diligently search for it. After much discussion, they had agreed to that concept.

"It's forming in my mind, Mr. Mayor," he informed the sometimes impatient city executive. "I have an appointment with Miss Helen tomorrow afternoon,"

"Don't waste your time with that old looney." The mayor reacted to the name of Miss Helen with a distasteful look probably because she had spoken out diligently against him in the last election. "That old bat can't remember where she was yesterday." The mayor's harsh words were probably a reference to her age which had to be past ninety and sometimes rumored to be closer to one hundred.

"Don't sell her short," Davis objected. "She may not remember yesterday, but she still has a vivid memory of what happed fifty years ago. Miss Helen still has more knowledge of this town in that ancient mind of hers than the rest of us put together. I am sure I can use some of the columns she wrote through the years. I just hope she still has them because I haven't been able to find copies elsewhere," Davis added.

"If you say so, but I wouldn't count on her too heavily," the mayor grunted when he walked past Davis to his destination.

After his visit with Carol which did include a cup of her tea, Davis wandered back down the street to his own shop where he committed himself to the tasks at hand. Without distractions, he stayed extremely busy for the next couple of hours. Ultimately, he decided he needed a light lunch before he met Charley at one thirty. Davis got in his Jeep to drive out to the Subway. By the time he got inside, one of the ladies had already made his sandwich.

"Saw you when you got out of your car," she said. "The daily special on wheat, no cheese, toasted with lettuce, tomato, black olives, pickles, banana peppers, spicy mustard, and vinegar, right?"

Davis thought of Brenda and the boys at the Little Rock.

With a full stomach Davis arrived in front of Charley's apartment at almost precisely one thirty. He was almost out of the Jeep when he saw Charley who rapidly walked toward him, so he got back in. When Charley was buckled in, he told the driver, "It's nice to have a chauffeur for a change rather than be a chauffeur."

"This is your first ride in my Jeep, isn't it?"

"That's right, and may I suggest that you get a real car or maybe a pickup? There is not a lot of room in this excuse for a vehicle, and its ability to handle any kind of load is almost zero. I bet you can't get this heap to go ninety downhill. How will you catch the bad guys in a buggy like this?"

"You forget, as my daughter often reminds me, I am a bookman, not a policeman. I don't intend to catch any lawbreakers. That is your job. I will overlook your remarks because I know you are just jealous. You know you would love to drive around in a beautiful vehicle exactly like this one."

"I'm not very smart, but I'm not dumb either. I'm saving my money for a fancy sports car that is capable of at least one hundred sixty or maybe a nice giant-sized pickup. One will impress the chicks; the other will leave the good old boys in awe. What did you say is the name of this realtor we are about to interview?" Charley suddenly changed the course of the conversation.

"He is Kerry Austin, a friend of mine and Amy's from church. He was the logical choice when Jay and Amy decided to search for a place to buy. I don't know him extremely well, but he seems to be a nice guy."

"You think everyone is a nice guy. You need to wake up and realize that at least half the population in this world is out to get you or to get what you have," Charley declared.

"Your time as a cop has made you cynical. Everyone has faults, but that doesn't make them bad people. I bet even you have a few flaws, but that doesn't mean you are a creep out to sucker every one with whom you come into contact."

"You're right, I did have a couple of faults at one time in my life, but that was a long time ago and I have long since conquered them," Charley stated with a laugh.

The two men on a mission drove along the old Dixie Highway past the high school and middle school complexes to turn right at the Stoner Baptist Church. They traveled another couple of miles before they pulled into the driveway of a newer home beautifully landscaped.

"Real estate agents must do all right," Charley said, surveying the elaborately landscaped yard.

"Realtors are like most people: those that work hard do all right, and those who don't struggle," Davis submitted before he opened the door to exit the Jeep.

Kerry greeted them at the door where Davis apologized for their interruption on a Saturday afternoon. "I know it would have been better for us to make an appointment to meet you at your office on a weekday, but we were pushed for time. Kerry, this is Charley Nelson. He is one of our Adairsville policemen."

"Yes, I have seen Charley around, but I don't believe we have ever actually been introduced." Kerry extended his hand to the young policeman in civilian clothes who took it.

"We won't keep you away from whatever you are busy with for very long," Davis told the realtor who was dressed in work clothes. "Jay and Amy told me that a man by the name of Johnson made an offer on the Ammon farm shortly after they submitted their offer. Can you give me any information about that man?"

"Not much, I'm afraid. He came by the office to tell us he was ready to sign a contract. I never even showed him the property. He assured me he was well acquainted with it, which seemed a little strange since he was from out of town. He was somewhat disturbed, almost angry, when he learned that an offer had already been accepted on the house and acreage. When he realized it had not been finalized, he announced he would top the previous offer even though he knew no details of that contract. I called the owners but, as you no doubt know, they felt obligated to Jay and Amy, so they rejected his offer—and that seemed to infuriate him even more. He left the office muttering about people who did not have any sense of how to do business."

"You said he was from out of town," Charley interjected; "Do you know where he is from?"

"I'm not sure, but one remark he made caused me to think he was from either North or South Carolina. I could be wrong about that?"

"Can you describe him for us?" Davis asked,

"Well, I'll do the best I can; I tend not to be very observant. I guess he was of average height, maybe six feet tall and a little on the chunky side. I would say he is middle-aged, maybe somewhere between forty-five and fifty-five. His hair is a bit grey and a little thin on top. He was dressed in a dark suit and white shirt, but no tie."

"That is a pretty good description for someone who is not very observant," Charley offered. "Did you notice any unusual characteristics—the way he walked, spoke, or maybe any distinguishing marks such as scars or such?"

"No, I remember nothing like that, but as I said I'm not very observant."

"One more question and we will get out of your hair," Davis told the realtor. "Did you get his first name?"

"Yes; as I remember, it was Reed; Reed Johnson was the name he gave me." Kerry seemed pleased that he remembered and, at the mention of that name, Davis glanced at Charley who knowingly looked back at him.

The two investigators got back into the Jeep to travel to Waleska for their second interview. Even before they got out of Kerry's driveway, Davis asked Charley, "Did you catch that? Mr. Johnson's first name is Reed! That is the name the waitress said our tattooed man used to refer to his friend at the restaurant. And the description certainly is similar to the one the waitress gave us."

"Yeah, I heard that. We assumed Reed was a last name, but maybe it was a first name."

"That is, no doubt, what your girlfriend out at the motel thought when she checked the records. Have her look to see if there was a Reed Johnson there when Juan Norris was registered."

"You know that even if we find that they were there at the same time and ate dinner together, it doesn't mean there is any connection. They could have been in town for different reasons without ever having met one another, but got to be friends after they became acquainted at the motel," Charley cautioned.

"Maybe, but that sounds like a lot of coincidence to me," Davis reasoned. "Let's first find out if Reed Johnson and Juan Norris were together, and then we can go from there. Do you remember that the gas station attendant said Norris questioned him about a cave east of Adairsville? And Johnson was interested in property east of Adairsville that is rumored to have a cave? I guess it could be a coincidence, but it seems to me to be a little too much to call it that."

"We should get to Waleska in about twenty-five or thirty minutes," Davis informed Charley when they turned right onto Highway 140 in the direction of the small college town. "Tom Landerhorn is an educator. He is a full-blooded Cherokee with a PhD in Native American studies, but his specialty is Cherokee culture. I have never met anyone who has a better grasp of the history and customs of that tribe."

"How did you meet him?" Charley questioned Davis while he looked at his cell phone to see who was ringing him. He chose not to take the call and turned his phone off to put it back into his pocket.

"He came by the shop one day to ask for my help to find a rather rare book. For years he has been searching for a first edition copy of *History of the American Indians* by Irishman James Adair published around 1770."

"Is that one of the Adairs that Adairsville is named for? I've always heard they were Irish and lived among the Cherokees."

"I believe they were Irish, and I have heard it said that James who wrote the book may actually be the father of those two who married Cherokee women and eventually were chiefs of sorts among the people of that tribe. However, the research I have done tells me that was not the case. There may have been some kind of family connection, but I don't think they were direct descendants of the author.

"I have read excerpts from a later copy of his book. He traveled among the Catawba, the Creeks, the Choctaws, the Chickasaws, as well as the Cherokees. His exposure to various tribes makes it an interesting read for anyone wanting to know about the Southeastern tribes.

"I guess it is because of my theological background that I am fascinated by his premise. Adair believed the American Indians are actually the descendants of the ancient Jews—the ten lost tribes. And he makes some pretty convincing arguments such as the fact that before Native Americans were exposed to the white man and his Bible, there was a tradition of a huge number of braves who crossed a great river on dry ground led by a man whose name translates into English as Moses."

"You're not going to preach to me now, are you?" Charley asked.

"Don't worry. I have no sermon prepared for you today, but if you ever decide you want to talk about spiritual matters, I stand ready to oblige you."

"Don't plan that conversation for anytime soon. I have more important matters to attend to, but if or when it happens, you will be the man," Charley told him.

Lord, I know you can speed that time up. May it be soon. Charley so needs you in his life, Davis prayed silently. "I think we are just about there. I've never been to Tom's house but according to the directions he gave me, we turn right at the four-way stop and go about a half mile where we will find his home on the right."

The two followed directions and found the log house exactly where they had been told it would be. After Davis introduced Charley to Dr. Landerhorn, he turned to his host.

"We do appreciate you taking time to see us today, and we will try to be brief. I know you are an important man who has lots to do," Davis spoke as he tried to take in all the fascinating things that were in the large room.

"I see you are interested in my collection," Tom observed the attention Davis gave to the displayed items. "These things are part of a collection that I began over thirty years ago. They are almost all Cherokee artifacts. Those are broken pieces of pottery I had mounted and framed, and here are some arrowheads, baskets, stickball gear, decorated gourds, masks, and weapons. I even have a few pieces of authentic clothing. Out on the back porch I have a canoe cut out of a cypress tree."

"Wow, that is impressive! All that must have cost you a small fortune." Davis immediately regretted that inappropriate remark.

"No, I paid for very little of my collection. Most of it I dug out of the ground or picked up off the top of the ground."

"It looks to me as if you have your own museum here. Let me show you why we are here." Davis pulled from a file folder the enlarged picture of the symbols on the chest and stomach of the tattooed corpse.

"We believe these markings are from the Cherokee alphabet. We need you to confirm that and see if you can interpret it for us."

The learned Native American gentleman sat down on the sofa and laid down the picture on the table in front of him. He took a pair of glasses from his shirt pocket and put them in place so as to see the details. He studied the picture for a few moments before he grabbed a legal pad and pencil from the table. He looked at the picture again before he scribbled a few words and repeated the process several times before he turned to his two visitors to tell them, "You are absolutely right. The symbols on this man's chest are indeed from the Cherokee syllabary. It seems to be directions to an object or destination that is not named." The Cherokee scholar then paused and continued to look at the picture.

"Exactly what does it say?" the impatient Charley asked his host.

"Translated it says that the location of that in question can be found just off the Pine Log Trail between the villages of Oothcalooga and Pine Log. A turn south is to be made at the place of the five large rocks, and five hundred fifty paces will lead to the bottom of the hill where a tree with a mark that looks like an s marks the spot."

Davis wrote Tom's exact words on a pad he brought with him.

"Does that make sense to you?" Tom asked. "I suspect you know that the village of Pine Log was just west of here on the way back to Adairsville. The little community of Pine Log was named for that significant village, and Oothcalooga was the village from which Adairsville grew when the Cherokees were moved west. That probably means whatever was sought was probably somewhere around the little community of Folsom."

"It is starting to make some sense," Davis told him.

"I don't want to be nosy, but I have to ask," Tom interjected, "Why were these directions tattooed on a man's chest?"

"I wish we knew," Davis responded. "The really strange turn of events is that the man with the tattooed directions is actually a visitor from Brazil of all places. Go figure!

"When we put it all together, maybe we can fill you in," Davis said. "You have been extremely helpful. When I have more time I would love to return to take a close look at your collection as well as pick your brain a bit about Cherokee history."

"You will be welcome anytime," his friend told him. "Have you found that book for me?"

"No, I haven't. You gave me a really tough assignment, but I promise you I will leave no stone unturned. If it is available, we will find it."

"Let's sum up what we know," Charley suggested to Davis on their way back to Adairsville. "We know that a Brazilian citizen with directions to a location near Folsom died of natural causes in Adairsville while he looked for a cave. His body was stolen from the funeral home and then dumped out on Woody Road. While still alive, he may have had contact with a man by the name of Reed Johnson who was unhappy that Jay and Amy made an offer on a farm in Folsom that prevented him from purchasing it himself. We know that Jay was rather forcefully warned by two thugs not to buy the farm. Does any of that add up?"

"Dim though it may be, a picture is starting to emerge. Obviously, we still need a few more pieces; however, there is no doubt we have made some progress today."

"We need to get home," Charley declared. "I have a date with Debbi, the clerk at the motel, and I don't like to be late for first dates. By the way, I will get my pilot's license next Tuesday."

"The friendly skies will no longer be friendly," Davis joked with his friend.

"And you have a big day ahead too. Isn't Amy's wedding scheduled for next Saturday? How do you feel about your little girl getting married?"

"I don't much like change, but the fact is, at this point in my life, my biggest concern is for Amy's happiness and safety. Jay makes her happy, so I am elated that they have found each other. I thank God every day for him."

"That's not what you said a few months ago. I thought maybe you were ready to put a contract out on him."

"That shows you how selfish and inconsiderate an old preacher can be. I rejected Jay earlier because his love for Amy was changing my relationship with her, and I didn't much like that. I have finally come to realize that if I am to find any peace of mind, I will have to accept the fact that I can't always keep things exactly the way I want them. It is called 'adjusting.'"

"Does that mean you have reconsidered the possibility of a future with Deidre? There is no doubt in my mind she adores you, and it is obvious you feel the same way about her. Don't you think it is time the two of you came to an agreement?"

"I don't know, Charley. Yes, I do have a strong affection for her, but I don't know if it is fair for me to saddle her with my hang-ups, and, of course, there is the age difference. But despite that, my desire to have her as a permanent part of my life seems to grow stronger each day. But then I don't even know how she feels about that."

"You will never know if you don't ask her," his friend with the uncomplicated, head-first philosophy of life told him. "Could that strong affection that you are talking about be called maybe ... uh ... love?"

The talk of Deidre caused Davis's foot to get a little heavier on the accelerator. He expected that she and her friends would have arrived next door when he got home, and that made him extremely happy.

CHAPTER 7

After he dropped Charley off at his apartment, Davis arrived home to see a small U-Haul truck backed into the driveway where several people were unloading furniture and boxes. Amy's things had been moved around the corner to the little house on College Street, and now most of Barbara Mason's belongings were in the apartment. The busyness of the scene reminded Davis of Friday nights at the high school football stadium. Anxiously, he looked for Deidre. She was not visible outside, so he hurried inside. He greeted the workers as he passed, "Hi, guys. That looks like hard work."

When Davis entered the house, he heard voices in Deidre's living room and headed in that direction. His eyes immediately focused on Deidre with that familiar ponytail that hung almost to her shoulders. She wore the jeans and T-shirt he had often seen her wear when there was work to be done. Before she turned to catch sight of him, his thoughts were, *Even dressed for work, she is the most beautiful woman I've ever known.* Immediately he thought of the beautiful Julie, the apple of his eye for so many years, and felt guilty for his thoughts.

When Deidre saw Davis, she scurried across the room and put both arms around his neck to tightly hug him. "It is good to be home. I've missed you so!" It sounded like she meant it.

"And I've missed you. It seems like you have been away for at least a month," he told her.

Deidre held Davis's hand as she pulled him over to the side of the room from which she had come. There were two people there he had not even noticed a few moments earlier. Deidre's radiance, he decided, had blocked out their presence. "Barbara, this is Davis Morgan, our landlord, and Davis this is, Barbara Mason, your new tenant. I know the two of you will be great friends."

Even a simple introduction seemed so elegant coming from Deidre. "It is good to meet you, Mrs. Mason. Deidre has told me enough about you to leave me with no doubt she is right, we will be good friends. Welcome to Adairsville."

"Please, call me Barbara. Good friends ought to be on a first-name basis. I want you to meet my son," the proud mother presented her good-looking offspring to her new landlord. "Ted came along to help me get settled. He lives in Savannah."

"I've looked forward to meeting you since I learned you would accompany these ladies. I'm glad you were along to look out for them on the trip. Deidre told me your skill kept the two of you from possible injury in the accident. I thank you for that." The two men greeted one another with a handshake and more intense eye contact than normal. "How long will you be with us?" Davis questioned the erect young man who stood before him.

"I have arranged to take all of next week off, but I don't know how long I will hang around here. I'll just play it by ear and see how it goes," Ted answered as he glanced toward Deidre.

Davis felt as if he needed to offer his spare room to Ted, but he was reluctant to do so because he did not know whether Amy had decided to stay with the ladies in her old apartment or take his guest room while she waited for the big day yet a week away. *Or was it just plain old jealousy that kept him from offering the young man a bed?* he wondered.

"Jay invited me to stay with him for a few days." Ted's remark eliminated Davis's guilt. "His hospitality gives me some flexibility.

And I guess someone needs to stay with him to help keep his nerves intact as he anticipates the wedding." Ted laughed at his own feeble attempt at humor.

In another half hour the truck was unloaded with everything inside the apartment, but not entirely placed in an orderly fashion. "We can do that later, after Barbara has had enough time to decide where she wants everything," Deidre told those who stood around trying to catch their breath.

"And then she will want to move it all again every day for about a week before she is finally happy," remarked Ted who had experienced several moves with his mother.

The three young men who had helped with the work excused themselves in favor of other Saturday night activities. That left the three people who had arrived from South Georgia along with Davis, Jay, and Amy.

"Looks like we will have six for dinner. We need to make some plans," Amy told her father. "We have everything we need for sandwiches except bread. I can make a salad. Dad, why don't you run to the grocery store for some sandwich bread, chips, and maybe a couple of desserts? That will simplify the process, and we can sit around and eat to our heart's content while we catch up on lost time."

"I'll go with you to help you pick out the desserts," Deidre told him.

When they went through the front door onto the big porch, she lifted her head to spot Davis's new vehicle for the first time. "You got your Jeep!" she cried out excitedly. "When did you get it?"

"I bought it the day after you left for South Georgia, but it was the day after that before I got to drive it home. I don't know that buying a new vehicle was such a good idea at this particular time, but my old Ford, as you know, was just about on its last leg, and I have wanted a Jeep forever. While in the ministry a Jeep just wasn't practical, but now seems to be the right time."

"Well, I think it's great. I'm glad you finally did something for yourself."

Deidre's approval made Davis feel better about his decision. It was always that way with Julie. Whether it was a decision about an automobile or some other purchase, he was never comfortable until his wife expressed her approval, which she almost always did.

It took only a few minutes for Davis and Deidre to get what they needed from the grocery store and make their way through the checkout line. When he drove out of the parking lot, Davis, as the law requires, came to a complete stop before he entered Highway 140. A white pickup passed in front of them and Davis noticed the man who sat in the passenger seat.

"That's Stringbean!" he almost shouted. "I'm sorry, but I've got to follow him." Davis pulled out behind the pickup truck. He was careful to follow far enough behind as not to be spotted. He could see there were three men in the truck which had a second seat. "The driver is, no doubt, the Sumo Wrestler, but I wonder who the third man is?"

"What is this all about?" Deidre asked. "Who are Stringbean and the Sumo Wrestler?"

"I'll explain later," he said as they drove north on Highway 41. They passed the city limit sign and a few hundred yards later crossed over into Gordon County headed toward Calhoun. *It will do no good to call the Adairsville Police. They have no jurisdiction here, and what will I tell the Gordon County authorities? They'll probably think I'm out of my mind.* "I just need to see where they are going," he told Deidre. One car remained between them and the pickup as they continued to follow.

The vehicle traveled about five miles which put them alongside the Calhoun Airport. Suddenly the driver of the pickup turned on his left blinker and almost immediately made a left turn into the small airport compound.

"We had better not follow them in there. They would spot us for sure," Davis spoke more to himself than to Deidre. "We'll turn right into this lot across the highway and wait for them to return, then we can pick them up again."

"What if they don't return anytime soon?" Deidre asked. "They might be in there for hours."

"That is not likely, but if it happens we will go home. I'll just come back later to see what I can learn about their being here. Those are the two guys who threatened to hurt Jay if he did not pull out of the Ammon farm deal. If we can learn where they are held up, the police can take it from there."

Five or six minutes later the white pickup reappeared at the gate and headed south back toward Adairsville. Davis started up his engine to pull out behind them, but this time there was no car between them. He noticed that he could see only two heads through the rear windshield. That caused him to conclude that a passenger had been dropped off at the airport. That struck him as a little odd since it was not generally a commercial facility.

After a mile or so, the two thugs evidently figured out they were being followed. The Sumo Wrestler stomped the accelerator and in a matter of moments the pickup sped down the road at a rate that would have served a Daytona 500 driver well.

"They will get away!" Deidre cried. "Speed up or you will lose them."

"No, I'll not take that chance with you in the car. They are not that significant. My suspicion is their threats were just bluffs. Their job is to apply enough pressure to enable whoever paid them to get what he wants. They aren't important enough to risk that kind of speed."

"It's not me you are worried about. You just don't want to do any harm to this shiny new Jeep." Perhaps because of his strong feelings for Deidre, her attempt to lighten the moment did not go over well with Davis, but to hide it, he managed a quick insincere chuckle.

Davis took the seven or eight minutes needed to get back home to give Deidre the brief version of the previous few days' events. She quietly listened with her mouth open before she finally asked, "How do you get yourself into these messes?"

When they arrived back at the house, there were some questions about where they had been. Not wanting to alarm the others, they had agreed that they would not tell them about the Springbean-Sumo Wrestler adventure, at least not now. Ted seemed especially curious about where they had spent their time while away from the others.

Amy opted to remain with Deidre and Barbara for what one of the ladies termed, the "girls slumber party." That was exactly what it sounded like across the hallway. Davis could hear a lot of laughter and loud conversation that reminded him of some of the overnight events that Amy hosted in their home as a teenager. He was delighted the three ladies could enjoy themselves.

Davis was about ready to fall asleep in his old comfy but worn-out chair that Julie had purchased for him on his thirty-eighth birthday when his cell phone rang. He answered with, "Hello," before he heard Charley's voice.

"I hope I didn't wake you. I know you senior citizens like to hit the hay early, but I needed to know if Deidre finally made it home?" Charley asked his friend.

"She is home and well. In fact, it sounds like there are at least ten of them next door in the middle of a rowdy party."

"Maybe I ought to look in on them to make sure they keep it down. That is the sort of work cops do, you know."

"You stay away from there or I will get my shotgun out. All wolves that show up around here after ten o'clock will be shot and skinned," Davis said, laughing.

"I thought I would let you know that Debbi and I stopped by the motel to check the records. We found no Reed Johnson, but we did find an R.T. Johnson from Franklin, North Carolina, who has been a guest of the motel three times in the last six weeks. One of those stays would have been while Juan Norris, our tattooed man, was registered. I have no doubt that Reed Johnson and R.T. Johnson from Franklin, North Carolina, are one and the same."

"You're probably right. Let me give you my report. When Deidre and I went to the grocery store early tonight, I spotted Stringbean and his sidekick, the Sumo Wrestler. They were in a white Ford pickup with a third man as a passenger. We followed them undetected to the Calhoun airport where they unloaded their passenger. Unfortunately, they spotted us when we tried to follow them back toward Adairsville and got away. Since I cautiously lay back, we never got close enough to get the license plate number or even know for sure if they had Georgia plates."

"I don't know of anyone around town that would come close to matching your description of those two. They must be from out of town. I will hit all the motels around town tomorrow to see if anybody knows who they are. I will also run by the Calhoun airport to see if I can get any information about the man your friends dropped off there. Since I will be a little out of my element in Gordon County, I doubt I will have a lot of success unless I find a beautiful female there. Gorgeous girls always seem to want to help me," Charley bragged. "You be careful. You really don't have any business following anyone, especially guys with guns. Watch your step," Charley told him. "Remember that you are a bookseller and not a cop."

Charley hung up before Davis could tell him that people have often reminded him of that. "You have a nice evening too," Davis sarcastically said to the dead air on the other end of the line before he put his phone back into his pocket. *I wish he would quit that!*

Jay and Ted took a little time to get acquainted before they turned in. "How long have you lived in Adairsville?" Ted asked his host.

"I've just now started to settle in," Jay told Ted who was a few years older than himself. "Just about everything I have is still in Orlando. My company transferred me to Atlanta, and I am to start work there one week after we are married. We will fly to Orlando where we will spend our honeymoon. We plan to drive home a U-Haul loaded with my stuff from my Florida apartment, but not until after we have basked in the sun for a few days."

"That won't be much of a honeymoon for you since you have been living there."

"Oh, that doesn't matter. Orlando is still new to Amy, and, regardless of the location, a honeymoon with Amy is still a honeymoon. The location isn't important."

"You are a lucky man. Obviously the two of you are very much in love. I wonder about Davis and Deidre's relationship. Are they an item?" he asked his host.

"Oh, I don't know. They seem to be very good friends, but I don't know that it is romantic. I really haven't thought too much about it."

Ted excused himself to the bedroom he had been assigned. He lay awake and listened to every sound around him for most of the night. *A couple more days and they will be on to me. The auditors will have done their job and I will be a goner. I don't know whether to keep on going north or go back to face the music. I don't know if it really matters. Life is not worth living anyway. It's all a sham.*

CHAPTER 8

A t nine thirty the big bell rang from the church on top of the hill. A little later, the group of six people took two vehicles to the service. The music was exceptional—a blend of contemporary and traditional songs, an innovation Pastor John had been able to install since he began his ministry with the church. Mrs. Parker, a lady with a terrific voice, sang a magnificent rendition of "How Great Thou Art" just before the sermon. The beautiful music prepared Davis to hear the sermon, and John did not disappoint.

Davis knew the young preacher, in his first pastorate, to be an exceptional communicator for a man so young with such limited experience, but he outdid himself on this particular Lord's Day. The tall young speaker in the pulpit spoke of the true nature of discipleship. He called the attention of the congregation to several hard sayings of Jesus about how to be his follower. John quoted the words of Jesus in Luke 14:25–27:

Large crowds were traveling with Jesus, and turning to them he said: 'If anyone comes to me and does not hate his father and mother, his wife and children, his brothers and sisters – yes, even his own life—he cannot be my disciple. And anyone who does not carry his cross and follow me cannot be my disciple.'

"Didn't Jesus know when he had it good? Large crowds followed Him, but He did just the opposite of what it takes to keep a crowd," the preacher explained. "Jesus knew how to whittle down a congregation. He talked with them about the need to place Him above even their own families. He told them to carry a cross. Who carried a cross in Jesus' day? It was those who were about to be executed—those about to be put to death. They carried their own cross to the place of execution. So Jesus told that crowd and He told us, 'If you would be my disciple, you have got to be willing to give up any distraction that would cause you to give Me less than first place, and you must even die for Me if called upon to do so.' That's hard, isn't it? But that is what Jesus said."

The insightful preacher went on to remark, "If you take those hard sayings of Jesus, put them in a bag, shake and mix them, you will come away with four important principles." He took the remainder of his sermon time to talk about what he saw as the four principles of discipleship: a complete trust in the Master; a refusal to be distracted from the purpose given to us by the Master, commitment to do whatever it takes to be like the Master, and, like the Master, be more concerned about the needs of others than our own desires. His final statement was, "As disciples of Jesus, our submission to Him must be total."

Perhaps because of guilt, Davis, for a time after he left the ministry, found it hard to sit through sermons, but he had learned to appreciate the messages of his young pastor. He found the Biblical content and practical application to be very helpful to his own life.

"Where will we go for lunch?" Amy asked after they exited the church building.

"I thought we were to eat at your apartment. Haven't you prepared Sunday lunch for all six of us?" Davis teased, glaring seriously at his daughter before he flashed a big smile. "I guess it is either the Adairsville Inn or Cracker Barrel," he conceded.

"I vote Cracker Barrel," Amy voiced her opinion. "It has greater variety and it costs less."

"Cracker Barrel it is then," Davis decided. "See if you can round everyone up and we will head in that direction."

Since a large crowd had chosen the popular restaurant for Sunday lunch, there was a thirty-minute wait to be seated. The delay enabled the group to assemble on the front porch to take advantage of the rather hot but beautiful blue sky day with which the little North Georgia town had been blessed. The three ladies took the three rocking chairs that were not occupied, while the men stood to wait their call to the dining room.

"Tell me about Adairsville," Ted turned his attention toward Davis as he spoke. "What is special about this town?"

"You may regret that question," Davis responded, suddenly lighting up. "The history of Adairsville is one of my favorite subjects. I've been known to elaborate on it for hours at a time.

"We had our start less than two miles north of our present location near what is today the Bartow/Gordon county line. A Cherokee Indian village known as Oothcalooga was located there. A family of Scotch-Irish adventurers by the name of Adair found a home with the Cherokee, a couple of them chose Cherokee wives, and eventually became chiefs. They went west to Oklahoma along with the others at the time of the removal that has come to be known as the Trail of Tears."

When Davis paused, Ted asked, "So how did the town end up at its present sitet?"

"When the state railroad was built, the governor chose a spot halfway between Atlanta and Chattanooga to locate the terminus which prompted him to build large machine shops just south of what once had been the site of the Indian village. With the development of the terminus, naturally the settlers moved their homes and businesses near the newly developed spot. It was incorporated in 1854 as Adairsville to honor the Scotch-Irish chiefs who had once lived nearby. We are a railroad town. That is why our business section faces the railroad."

With his curiosity aroused or perhaps to keep the conversation on a roll, Ted suggested, "Give me some of the historical high points."

"Well, several significant events have occurred though the years, but I think you would be more interested in some of the people who once called Adairsville home. On a high hill to the west one can see a house that is called High Lonesome. A young man by the name Carl Boyd grew up there in the late nineteenth and early twentieth century. He went on to graduate from West Point and became a world-class horseman. Eventually he became a colonel on General Pershing's support staff through most of World War I. He is the officer who gave the cease fire command that ended the war. Shortly thereafter he died of influenza that swept through France. That young officer was on track ahead of almost all the men who became the great generals of World War II. Who knows how history would have been altered had he lived."

Davis stopped his speech to listen to the voice from the intercom. He hoped his party would be called to be seated; however, no such luck, so he continued his history lesson for the young South Georgia native.

"Since you are a preacher's son, you may recognize the name of Wally Fowler."

"No, I don't think so," Ted responded.

"Wally Fowler who grew up not far from where we now stand was Mr. Gospel Music, but his accomplishments went far beyond gospel music. He wrote great songs for people like Eddie Arnold, Frank Sinatra, Bing Crosby, and Pat Boone. He started a gospel group known as the Oak Ridge Quartet which later became the Oak Ridge Boys of country music fame."

"Morgan, your table is ready," the lady on the intercom announced. "Morgan party, please report to be seated."

"Ah, our table is ready, better get it while we can," Davis suggested.

Inside the restaurant, Davis stood back to allow everyone to find their place. They seated themselves boy–girl, and Davis was pleased when a seat for him was left next to Deidre while Ted seated himself beside his mother. When the waitress came to take orders, Davis chose the meat loaf.

As happens at so many Sunday dinners, the conversation turned to the sermon. "What did you think about the message today?" Jay, who up to this point had remained rather quiet, asked. "I normally love John's sermons, but it seemed to me he was just a little unreasonable today."

It was his fiancée who responded, "I believe we have gotten so far away from the true Biblical concept of discipleship that on those rare occasions when its true nature is held before us, we see what should be normal as radical."

A father could not have been more proud of a daughter than Davis was of his at that moment. *She hit the nail on the head,* he thought. Davis decided to remain silent to see what the others would say on the subject.

"I was amazed at the insight of such a young man. It is apparent that he is an exceptional communicator. I think I will enjoy his Sunday sermons," Barbara commented.

Davis was glad to hear that Barbara expected to attend their services while she lived in Adairsville. *She will be a delightful addition to our church family*, he decided.

"Because my dad was a preacher I have sat through an awful lot of sermons, and I have more often than not highly respected the men who presented those sermons. That includes my father," Ted told the group around the table. "But it seems to me that most of what I hear has very little to do with real life. I think too much of what is presented from the pulpits is about what we need to do rather than how to find the help we need."

After that remark, Davis wanted to jump in to defend his young pastor friend. He felt there was no more practical preacher to be found anywhere than John, but he refrained. The former preacher knew Ted was not talking about John as much as he was about himself. Davis concluded that this sad young man evidently had some real unfulfilled needs.

Across the table Davis observed that Barbara Mason dropped her head, but remained silent.

"John's sermons have been extremely helpful to me," Deidre spoke up. " He has helped me through a number of struggles, and I believe him to be an exceptional man of God. John's presentations come straight from the Word of God, and I happen to believe God has a pretty good handle on what we really need."

Amen! Davis thought, but stopped short of actually saying it. What a remarkable young woman Deidre was. *Not only beautiful and personable, but blessed with such strong spiritual insight. How is it possible that some guy has not camped on her doorstep until he won her heart?*

It was almost three o'clock when the six friends returned to the house which left Davis no time to change out of the suit and tie he wore before he visited with Miss Helen. *That's good,* he told himself. *Everybody knows that preachers wear suits or at least they did in Miss Helen's day.* His thoughts were triggered by recalling Helen Townsend's commitment to nag him into repentance over his "quitting the Lord," as she phased it. He had put his hand to the plow and turned back. Now it was her responsibility to help him see the error of his way. Maybe the suit would throw her off, he decided.

Davis knocked several times on the front door from Miss Helen's big front porch before he finally got her attention. "Miss Helen, did you remember our appointment?" he asked when she opened the door.

"Of course I did; I just fell asleep in my old easy chair. I hope you didn't have to wait too long," the dignified silver-haired widow apologized. "Come over here and take a seat." She directed him toward a big blue antique chair. "It is my most comfortable piece of furniture," she remarked as he was seated on the hardest seat in which he had ever sat. "I'll go get you some sweet tea." The aged lady slowly made her way to her kitchen.

Anyone who visited with Miss Helen was automatically served sweet tea. Davis did not object despite the fact his stomach was filled to capacity from the huge lunch he had just enjoyed. He knew that to protest would be pointless.

The gracious lady Davis had known all of his life returned after about five minutes with a white linen napkin. "You look like a preacher today," Miss Helen remarked in regards to his suit and tie.

In order to distract the sweet lady from where he saw the conversation going, Davis quickly jumped in to take control of its direction. "Miss Helen, the reason I am here is that the city officials have asked me to put together a history of our town. I know you are my best source for such information. With your permission, I would like to include in my book many of the columns you wrote in years past."

"I wrote hundreds of them," she informed him. "I did the Adairsville news for the *Journal* and the *Constitution*. You know they were once two separate papers, one the morning paper and the other the evening news. I did the same for the *Tribune* in Cartersville for more than fifteen years, and at various times I wrote columns for all three of the Adairsville papers. For a time, I even worked for the *News* over in Rome."

"I know you did, and I have read some of your stories. I would love to have as many of them as possible in the book. The problem is that I do not have access to that material. I wonder if you still have copies of your work, and, if so, would you give me permission to use it and let me borrow it long enough to make copies?"

"Why, certainly you have my permission, and you can keep it all for as long as you need, but I would eventually like to have it all returned," Miss Helen sternly stated.

"By all means," Davis responded. "I will take good care of your work and should be able to get it back to you in two or three weeks. I am sure as the process moves along I will have lots of questions that only you can answer. Will it be okay for me to call you again? This is a book that you probably should have written years ago."

"I often thought about that, but life always got in the way," Miss Helen replied, obviously pleased with Davis's words of praise. "Since I never got it done, I will do whatever I can to help you."

"I'm glad to hear you say that, Miss Helen, because I don't think it would be possible for me to compose such a book without you. I'm convinced you know more about the history of Adairsville than any person alive." Davis took a sip of his iced tea and then looked for a coaster on the nearby table where he could sit his glass. Not able to find one, he sat the glass on a magazine which was lying on the table.

"You flatter me, but I appreciate your praise. Adairsville has been my home for almost a century now. I have spent most of that time right here in this very house."

Davis could see from the distant expression on Miss Helen's face that her mind was about to go back to earlier times.

"Jonathan and I lived on South Main for three years, but after he passed I moved back here with Father and Mother, and I have been here ever since. It has been a good life, but because I never remarried, I have found myself rather lonely at times. Don't let that happen to you, young man!" Her manner was stern. "A pastor needs a good wife. The Lord has one for you, and you would do well to find her and latch on to her. Don't let her get away."

"I certainly take your advice seriously, Miss Helen. One more question," Davis requested after he took another sip of his sweet tea, "Can you tell me about the Ammon farm out near Folsom?"

"Why are you interested in that forsaken piece of property? It has sat unused for a good number of years I believe?"

"My daughter and her fiancé are about to buy the house with ten acres. I thought it might be helpful if you could tell me what you remember about it."

"Is the house still fit to live in? It has been in bad shape for years."

"Jay and Amy are convinced it is. Jay has some carpenter skills and they believe they can get it back in shape in six months' time or less."

"I guess they know what they are doing. I heard the cave was sealed years ago," Miss Helen reported.

"That is what I have been told. Do you remember anything about skeletons found in the cave?" Davis knew that if it had indeed happened, Miss Helen would know about it. He wiggled, trying to get a little more comfortable in Miss Helen's *soft chair*.

"Now that you mention it, I do remember that there was a rumor about that. I think it probably took place even before my time, but I remember my daddy talked about it. I think it was while World War I was in progress that Sam Ammon and one of his neighbors, maybe a Mr. Evans, dug up several complete skeletons that obviously had been buried in the cave for a long time. If I remember the story correctly, they took the bones to Dr. Dick Bradley who kept them in his office out at Folsom for months."

"What ultimately happened to the bones?" Davis inquired.

"I don't remember much about that part of the story," Miss Helen replied, "but it seems to me that maybe the doctor eventually gave them back to Mr. Ammon, and Sam took them somewhere back in the woods on his property to put back into the ground. I could be wrong about that part of the story."

"Do you know exactly where the cave is located in relation to the house?" the concerned father asked his normally reliable source.

"I believe it is less than a half mile directly behind the house. I can remember I was out there with a group of girls and boys when I was a girl. The boys went into the cave, but we girls stayed outside till they returned. I could be wrong about the distance, but I am sure it was directly behind the house."

"As usual, Miss Helen, you have been extraordinarily helpful. I can't tell you how much I appreciate your knowledge as well as your willingness to share it. I need to go, but could I take those copies of your columns with me?"

"Of course," she said. "You will need to go with me into the spare bedroom to retrieve them. They are heavy and my back isn't what it used to be." Davis was stunned when Miss Helen pointed to a box almost full of paper, large envelopes, and folders that sat in a corner of the room.

"I didn't realize there were that many," he said.

"I told you I wrote for several papers over a number of years. You will find most of it right there in that box," Miss Helen said as Davis leaned over to pick up the heavy cardboard box. "I hope you will find information you can use. By the way, I hope to hear you preach sometime soon," she told him as he left the front door with box in hand.

"I'll let you know the next time I fill a pulpit anywhere in town," Davis promised while he hurried across the porch. "I'll be in contact!"

After her guest left, Miss Helen sat to rest for a while before she prepared a snack for her evening meal. *I believe that boy will come around soon,* she thought. *I saw a sparkle in his eyes that has not been there since his wife passed. That boy will be back in the pulpit where he belongs preaching the gospel someday soon. And I wouldn't be surprised if we didn't hear about a new preacher's wife before long. I wonder who she is! I think I heard someone say he is sweet on that young history teacher.*

It had been a busy but enjoyable day for Davis. He could hear the voices of Jay and Ted in the apartment next door when he walked across his porch. The former preacher enjoyed the silence for a time and remembered that often ignored verse from Psalm 46:10, *Be still and know that I am God.* After an hour—or was it two?—he got up to go to the kitchen to make himself a roast beef sandwich which he ate with a few chips and a glass of water with lemon. After he satisfied his appetite, he moved back to his chair to start his journey through Miss Helen's columns. He soon discovered that this step in his research would not, at all, be a chore. He found himself sometimes fascinated, sometimes sad, and sometimes bent over with laughter. This was great stuff! But why would anyone expect less from a remarkable lady like Miss Helen?

CHAPTER 9

With his shop closed on Mondays, it was Davis's custom to use the day to search for the used and rare stock that kept his store relevant for booklovers throughout the area. He started his drive to Canton shortly after 8:30 a.m. About nine o'clock, Amy departed with Jay to go decorate and straighten up the little house they had rented temporarily. Shortly thereafter, Barbara and her son, Ted, drove away to spend some time together since they would soon be separated by a much longer distance than usual. Deidre was left in the large house all alone which she appreciated since there was house work to be done, a bridesmaid's dress to alter, and general catch-up made necessary by her recent time away.

With no one in my way, I ought to be able to make a dent in all the work, Deidre told herself. Then she heard the doorbell ring. *Who could that be? I'm not expecting anyone.*

Deidre strolled to the next room where she opened the front door to see two men through the screen: a tall skinny guy and a short, stout gentleman with a buzz haircut.

What could these guys want? Must be salesmen. I've never seen them before. Then she looked past the odd pair to see a white pickup in the driveway and something clicked. She remembered Davis's description of the tough guys who threatened Jay. *Stringbean and the Sumo Wrestler!* She panicked when she put two and two together. She turned to run without closing the door.

The screen door, the only obstacle between the frightened young teacher and the intruders, was latched from within. Stringbean kicked the frame and it sprang open. Both men ran after Deidre with Stringbean yelling, "Nowhere to go, Missy, you might as well make it easy." He caught her before she could get the back door open to make her escape. "Got you!" Stringbean laughed when he grabbed her from behind.

The tall ruffian needed the help of his stouter partner to get a secure hold on the desperate young woman who scratched, slapped, kicked, and screamed. They managed to drag her back through the house and out the front door to the pickup. They slammed her into the seat between them. Sumo Wrestler drove while Stringbean tried to tie a cloth of some kind across her eyes to serve as a blindfold. Deidre slapped it away.

The driver yelled, "That's enough!" He pulled a gun from his waistband, steering with his other hand. "Just calm down, lady, and you won't get hurt," he told her.

When Deidre saw the gun, she stopped her resistance and allowed the tall skinny guy on the other side to tie the blindfold. *Since they don't want me to know our destination, they must plan for me to return eventually,* she reasoned with a sigh of relief. Stringbean had not done a good job with the blindfold. She was able to have some vision when she tilted her head back and looked under it.

"Don't worry, Missy. If you and your boyfriend will cooperate, we will get you home in time for your wedding. We won't hurt you unless you make us," Stringbean assured her.

It was the reference to a wedding that caused Deidre to realize that these two dimwits thought she was Amy. In order to protect Amy, she decided she would tell them no different. As long as they were convinced they had Amy, her friend would be safe. She would go along with their game.

Deidre tilted her head back to look under the blindfold and saw that they were traveling along Shake Rag Road before they turned left onto Woody Road and then right at Oak Grove Church where they started across Brownlee Mountain. She sat quietly and was able to see that they crossed Highway 53 to go toward the little Plainville community. She assumed they had crossed the railroad in Plainville when she felt the rise of the vehicle. After a moment she took note that they turned right. The driver then took another right where she was able to see a cemetery. She knew exactly where she was. Four months earlier, she attended the burial of an elderly friend in this very cemetery.

The driver evidently saw the tilt of her head and realized she could see. "Check that blindfold!" he yelled at his partner. "Can't you get anything right?"

Stringbean adjusted the blindfold which kept her from seeing further, but she could vaguely recall the area in which she now knew they were, and she had a pretty good idea of their location when the truck stopped.

"Get out!" Sumo Wrestler yelled at Deidre. He seemed a little irate, perhaps because of the scratches she had left on his face in the earlier struggle. He roughly jerked the blindfold from her eyes. "This will be your home for now," the short, stocky man told her and then pointed to what seemed to be an abandoned house trailer that had long ago seen its better days.

"You are not about to put me in there!" Deidre objected.

"That is the plan, honey," Sumo Wrestler assured her.

There was a camper parked under a big oak tree fifty feet or so in front of the old abandoned mobile home. They had come to this spot on a dirt drive that looked as if it had almost been washed away by erosion. The area was pretty much surrounded by woods and undergrowth. She observed a lot of kudzu nearby. Deidre surmised that the camper was the lodging place for the two strange kidnappers—she decided the dumpy old house trailer wouldn't be too bad if it meant she would be separated from her creepy captors.

Sumo Wrestler herded Deidre toward the door of the dilapidated mobile home. He pushed her into the filthy trailer and looked around before he pulled a set of ancient blinds from the window they had been hung to cover. He lifted a pocket knife from his pocket and released the blade to cut some of the cord from the set of blinds.

"Turn around!" he harshly commanded the pale young lady with the weak knees. "Put your hands behind you. We need a little extra insurance since you like to fight." He used the cord to tie her hands behind her back.

"Ouch!" Deidre cried when her captor pulled the cord tight. "That hurts. You almost drew blood."

"Lady, this ain't a social gathering. You can expect to hurt a lot if you don't behave yourself," Sumo Wrestler threatened her as he nevertheless slightly loosened the cords around her wrists. After he made sure her wrists were securely tied, he led her to an old wooden straight chair, the only piece of furniture in the trailer, where he lowered her onto its hard seat. She wondered if the rickety piece of a chair would hold her weight. "You sit right here," he told her. He then pointed toward the other end of the trailer and announced with a chuckle, "The bathroom is down there." The man, perhaps five feet tall and well over two hundred and fifty pounds, took with him what was left of the cord from the blinds he had pulled off the window. He stepped outside, and she heard him fumbling at the door latch. Apparently he was using the cord to tie it shut.

Deidre looked around with disgust. She saw trash throughout the room in which she had been left. *No telling what is living here,* she thought, *probably fleas, bugs, and maybe even snakes. I've got to find a way out of here.*

She could hear the voices of her captors outside. She got up from the chair to slowly walk over to the window where she saw the two thugs set up a portable table under the shade of the big oak tree. Stringbean pulled two lawn chairs from their camper and placed one on each side of the small table before he reached into his shirt pocket to pull out a deck of cards.

"That is a right nice-looking girl," Deidre heard Stringbean say with a grin while he pointed toward the house trailer.

"You know what the boss said. You keep your hands off that girl," his partner reminded him.

"I know it. I was just looking," he responded before he again glanced toward the house trailer where Deidre was a prisoner.

He gives me the creeps; I've got to find a way out. Deidre continue to look around hoping to find an escape hatch. She remembered a passage of scripture John had used in a recent sermon, *And God is faithful; he will not let you be tempted beyond what you can bear. But when you are tempted, he will also provide a way out so that you can stand under it.* (I Corinthians 10:13). *Maybe a bit out of context since this isn't temptation, but it is surely a trial. God is still faithful—Lord, you have provided me a way out, I know you have. Please show me where it is.*

Sumo Wrestler talked on his cell phone but, with his back to her, Deidre couldn't hear what he said. Stringbean shuffled the cards. Deidre walked to the back of the trailer where she found another door and backed up to it in an effort to pull it open. It was useless. The knob would not turn. It was when she was walking away from the door that a large rat ran from a pile of trash across the floor, coming within inches of her feet. *Not rats!* she panicked, *I hate rats!. Anything but rats!* At that moment she decided, *I will not spend another hour in this horrible place.*

Deidre continued to explore her place of confinement by checking the windows in the back of the trailer. She stood on the chair to do so, but found them to be unmovable, *but perhaps she could break the glass.* She decided, however, if she did that, her captors were sure to hear. From time to time Deidre returned to the front window to check on the status of the two gamblers out front. They were still engrossed in their card game. She hoped that would continue for a while.

Still hoping to find an escape hatch somewhere, she reluctantly went into the bathroom to find it filthy beyond belief. She had taken only two steps into the room when the floor squeaked and slightly gave. It took every ounce of her willpower to drop her body onto the nasty floor, but when she did so, she was delighted to discover that the strips of wood that covered that part of the floor, at some time in the past, had been flooded enough to cause damage. For the next half hour, while Deidre's captors played cards not one hundred feet from her, she sat on the floor with her hands tied behind her and pulled away at the flooring.

There was some controversy among the captors resulting in a loud exchange that evidently caused the two villains out front to conclude their card game. Sumo went into the camper, announcing he was going to rest. "You keep watch," he told Stringbean. But in less than fifteen minutes, Stringbean was dozing in his lawn chair.

Deidre knew it was now or never. She said a quick prayer before squeezing through the small hole she had managed to create in the bathroom floor. She felt the spiderwebs against her face as she slowly slithered on her stomach with her hands still tied behind her. She wondered if there were spiders in those webs and cringed at the thought. *I'm almost sure there is at least one snake somewhere under this trailer. If our paths cross, he will not have to bite me. His presence alone will be enough to do me in. To run into a skunk, possum, or some other small animal would not, at all, surprise me.* She silently prayed, *Father, if ever I needed you, I need you now. Please, protect me.*

Deidre managed to make it to an opening in the back of the trailer underpinning and climb through it. She wished she could use her hands to brush the spiderwebs from her face and hair, but of course with them tied behind her, that was impossible.

She tried her best to keep the trailer between her and her two captors in order to stay out of their sight. Shortly after she got to the trees and bushes, she heard the two men cursing and yelling. She had been spotted, but she had a good start and continued to run as hard as she could through the kudzu that was sometimes more than waist-high. When she got through the kudzu, there were bushes and briars to contend with. She was now going downhill and could see a house at the bottom of that hill. She wondered if the kidnappers were still back there. She could not hear them, but that didn't mean they weren't right behind her. If she could make it to the house, maybe she would be safe.

She had once heard a preacher remark that when it started to hurt, we need to run a little faster. It hurt and she ran a little faster.

Jay and Amy were hard at work in the house in which they would live for a few months after they were married.

"I hear your cell phone," Amy informed her soon-to-be-husband who had left it on the table in the next room. Jay hurried in order to answer the phone before it stopped ringing.

"Jay, speaking," he announced when he put the cell to his ear. "Can I help you?"

"You sure can," the person on the other end of the line responded. Jay did not at first recognize the voice, but it did sound familiar. "You can call your realtor friend and tell him you are no longer interested in the Ammon property because, if you don't, your girlfriend, who we have right here with us, will find herself in big trouble."

There was now no doubt about the speaker. It was the short chunky guy who along with his skinny friend had accosted him. "You are bluffing. I know that because Amy is here with me at this moment. You guys are about to find yourselves locked up for an awfully long time if you don't back off. My advice to you is to get just as far away from Adairsville as you can go."

"I'm warning you, kid. Go check her apartment. We have her and you had best listen to what I tell you. You have until the end of the day to call that realtor or she will suffer greatly. You may never see her again if you don't follow my instructions." There was then only dead air on the other end of the phone.

By this time Amy stood beside her fiancé. "What's wrong?" She had heard his last words and observed the puzzled expression on his face.

"That was one of the men who threatened us not to buy the Ammon place. He told me he has you, and you are in big trouble if we don't call Mr. Austin to cancel our contract."

"Obviously, he is trying to pull a fast one since I am right here," Amy said. "Unless...."

Amy's face got pale and her eyes widened. "Unless they got Deidre thinking she is me. Let's go!" They ran out of the house toward the car in such a hurry they didn't even stop to lock the front door.

The moment Jay and Amy pulled into the driveway, they knew all was not right. The front door was wide open. When they sprinted in that direction, they saw that the screen door was in shambles.

"Deidre! Deidre!" Amy yelled as she ran from room to room. "They have her." Amy was now in a panic evidenced by the tears that streamed from her eyes. "They took her. They thought she was me. What will we do?"

"You call your dad and I'll call 911."

Davis was on his way home and had just passed the first Cartersville ramp when he received Amy's message. It was normally more than a twenty-minute drive home, but he was there in little more than fifteen minutes, his mind running wild all the way. *It is no telling what those monsters will do to her. Lord, you have got to protect her. Help us find her. Don't leave her out there somewhere with those half-wits. Lord, I can't lose her, too.*

Chief Hanson and Charley stood on his porch with Jay and Amy when Davis pulled into the driveway. Charley met Davis halfway across the yard. "She'll be all right," Charley assured him. "We will find her. And those snakes who took her are mine. They will not get away with this." Charley's red face and raised voice made him appear angrier than Davis had ever seen him. "Tell me what you can recall about the encounter you and Jay had with those guys."

"I think I have already told you all I remember, Charley; I just cannot think well right now. But I'll try. We've got to find her. We can't let anything happen to her."

Around 6:30 p.m., Davis was with Charley in an effort to cover all the streets in and around Adairsville. They looked for a white pickup truck that might belong to the kidnappers. "I know this is a long shot," Charley said, "but right now I don't know what else we can do."

"I know," Davis replied, "and I think I would go crazy sitting and waiting without doing something. I am grateful to Chief Hanson for letting me search with you."

"He's not all bad," Charley replied. "He knew you needed to be out doing something and that I wouldn't mind having you along. If we come across something, don't make me sorry I encouraged him to let you come. Remember that I am the policeman."

Davis had gotten a little tired of being reminded that he was not a policeman, but with his mind now on more important things, he did not even hear the reminder.

"Let's drive down the back streets in the St. Elmo area," Davis suggested. They covered those streets before checking behind the factory buildings on Patterson Lane, while again finding nothing helpful.

Then when they were stopped, ready to enter the Adairsville-Pleasant Valley Road, a white Ford pickup went past, headed north.

"Hang on!" Charley told Davis as he activated the lights and siren. Davis braced himself for a full-scale chase, but that didn't happen. The truck immediately pulled over and stopped. "You stay here," Charley instructed Davis as he walked toward the passenger side of the pickup with his hand on the top of his holstered pistol.

Davis watched closely, ready to do whatever he needed to do despite what Charley had told him. But after two or three minutes, Charley returned to his seat on the driver's side. "It was just Ralph Hayes," Charley told Davis. "I think I just about scared him out of his wits. How old is Ralph now? Maybe approaching eighty."

"I had forgotten that Ralph drives a white Ford pickup, but then there are a number of guys around town who do. How did you explain stopping him?"

"I just told him I wanted to say hello," Charley said, attempting to lighten the tension he and Davis were feeling.

"I don't know what I will do if anything happens to Deidre," Davis told his friend. "Other than Amy, she is the most special person in my life right now, and I don't know if I could live without her."

"I know how you feel," Charley said, hanging his head. "We will find her," Charley promised. *I hope with all my heart I can keep that promise.*

It was less than a half-hour later when Davis's cell phone rang from his pocket. "Hello," Davis said before he heard the sweetest sound he had heard in a long time.

"Davis, this is Deidre. You won't believe what I've been through, but I need to first tell you that I am fine—half scared out of my wits, but fine."

"We thought you had been kidnapped! What happened? Where are you?" In a matter of moments, Davis's emotions ran the gauntlet from relief to an uncertain fear.

"They took me, but I managed to get away," she told him. "I'm all right—really! Can you come and get me? I'm over in Plainville out on Miller Loop. Do you know where that is?"

"I'll find it," he assured her.

"I'll be in the home of some wonderful people named Medford who helped me. Their house number is 1008. You will see the number on the mailbox. They tell me there is a black iron gate across the drive, but it is open."

"We'll be there as quickly as we can get there," Davis told her before Charley turned on the siren and with blue lights flashing, they sped west toward Plainville.

It was no problem for Charley to find the Medford home located a couple of miles outside of the village. Deidre met them at the door where she hugged Davis tightly and didn't let go for a full four or five minutes before moving over to briefly embrace Charley. "I've never been more scared in my life," she calmly told them when they walked inside to meet and thank the Medfords.

"You don't know how grateful we are to you for the help you gave our girl," Davis directed his remarks to the middle-aged couple. "A lot of people would be extremely upset if any harm came to this special gal."

"When you find a young lady with the face of an angel at your door with her hands tied behind her back pleading for help, what else can you do? We only did what anyone else would have done," Harry Medford explained.

While there, Charley called the Gordon County Police department to see what he could learn about their investigation as a result of the Medfords' 911 call. He was told that by the time the authorities got to the trailer, the kidnappers had evidently hooked up their camper to make a clean getaway.

On the way back to Adairsville, Deidre shared the details of her escape from the kidnappers.

"I knew God had provided me with a way out when I walked into the bathroom and almost fell through the floor," she told them. "I was petrified because of what I might run up against under that trailer, but I knew I had to try."

Both Davis and Charley expressed their amazement at her composure under such pressure.

"I was scared to death," Deidre told them, "but somehow found the ability to keep going."

"I have always heard that courage is not the absence of fear, but the ability to keep going in the midst of fear," Davis added.

"I was a hysterical mess by the time I got to the Medfords' door. I've heard a lot of stories about people not wanting to get involved, but both of them came to the door, took me into their house, untied my hands, and called 911. They gave me water and took care of my cuts and bruises. What a blessing they were!"

"And even though intelligence isn't the strong suit of Stringbean or his pal, when they realized you had gotten away, they were smart enough to immediately pack up and get out of there as fast as they could," Davis surmised.

"The Lord worked it all out," Deidre told her two friends. "He is the one who protected me." She noticed that Charley turned to look at her and grew quiet after her last statement.

Jay and Amy along with Barbara and Ted met Davis and Deidre at the door, anxious to hear the details of what had happened.

"I'll tell you all about it tomorrow, but right now I've got to get a shower and some rest," Deidre pleaded before she headed toward her bedroom. By the time she got out of the shower and ready for bed, Jay and Ted had gone. Barbara and Amy respected her request and sat quietly in the living room while Davis had moved a chair into the hallway between the two apartments to put him in position to guard the ladies. He remained there throughout the night hearing every sound and only occasionally dozing. It was a long night for everyone in the big white house with the wraparound porch on the west side of Railroad Street.

CHAPTER 10

Anew day brought to Davis a cautious but more positive outlook despite the exhaustion he felt. Birds chirped and the sky was blue with an uncharacteristic late July breeze when he stepped out to the box beside his drive to get the paper. Most importantly, Deidre and Amy were safe in the apartment and unharmed. He thought of the words of one of his favorite verses which he memorized long ago,

"Weeping may remain for a night, but rejoicing comes in the morning. (Psalm 30:5)

One of the advantages of the Corra Harris Bookshop arrangement with the 1902 Stock Exchange was that there is always a clerk on hand to take care of the customers. That cost Davis ten per cent of his sales, but it made it possible for him to play hooky from his shop if he decided he wanted a day off. Today, he just wanted to stay home. He wanted to remain close to Amy and Deidre, to make sure they remained safe.

Davis showered and ate breakfast before sitting down to try to put the events of the previous day in perspective. In light of the obvious danger Amy and Jay were facing because of their decision to buy the old Ammon place, should he try to talk them out of it? *Maybe,* he decided.

What's the big deal about them getting that house. If calling the sale off will keep them safe, then that may be what they need to do. Besides, I don't even think it is their best deal. They can do better. But upon further reflection he concluded, *I don't need to make their decisions for them. They are young, but they are adults capable of making their own decisions. It would be wrong for me to set a pattern of imposing my will on them from the very beginning of their marriage. Maybe I will casually suggest to them that they can still back out, but let them decide. If they decide to go through with it, I will just have to keep a closer eye on them.*

Then there is the problem of Deidre's safety. If anything good came out of her abduction, it was that he was forced to admit to himself how much she meant to him. *I don't think I can live without her and maybe it's wrong, but I have an overwhelming desire to punish those heartless thugs who mistreated her if only I could get my hands on them.*

In an effort to try to get his mind off Stringbean and Sumo, Davis decided to try to filter through more of Miss Helen's columns. After he read several columns which dealt with religion in Adairsville, Davis picked up a folder marked "Civil War-Related."

Miss Helen's take on 'The Great Locomotive Chase' which gave the account of perhaps the most famous train chase of all time caught Davis's attention. It was the account of the Texas chasing the General that had been stolen by Yankee spies. The pursuit went right through Adairsville. The General ran out of fuel just north of Ringgold where the Raiders scattered and most of them were captured. Miss Helen naturally wrote her column on the subject from the Confederate perspective. She praised Captain Fuller and the Texas which she reported ran backwards at nearly sixty miles an hour along track posted at sixteen miles an hour.

After he read that account and got a chuckle over Miss Helen's obvious bias, Davis picked up a folder marked "Reconstruction." He pulled out a page entitled "Confederate Soldiers in Brazil." His interest was piqued because he recalled the tattooed body he and Charley found was that of a man from Brazil. The article was about some Confederate soldiers and their families who settled in Brazil after the war in order to get away from the desolation and cruelty of reconstruction. After he read several paragraphs, Davis came to this passage:

By 1870, Santa Barbara, Brazil, had many representatives from the South. Among them from Georgia were Dr. George Barnsley and Lucian Barnsley, sons of Godfrey Barnsley, who eventually settled at San Paulo where George married Mary Lamira Emerson. Most of the Confederates were planters, and settled on rich farm lands to plant cotton and other seeds brought from the wrecks of their former homes.

It was not long until there were over five hundred Southern families who lived in Villa Americana alone, while thousands took up abode at other sites. The greatest handicap for most of them was the Portuguese language. That was overcome in time. With diligence, ingenuity, and hard work, the majority became adapted to their alien surroundings. The headstones in cemeteries located in places like Santa Barbara bear the names of soldiers from general down to private. The deceased names give evidence of many Adairsville connections like Barnsley, Emerson, Swain, Burns, and Norris....

Davis did a double take, "I don't believe it!" Davis spoke aloud even though no one else was in the room. *Charley has got to see this! Santa Barbara is the name of the tattooed man's home town and Norris was his name. Could it be coincidence? I doubt it!*

This bit of news, at least momentarily, took Davis's mind away from yesterday's events. He took his cell phone from his pocket to call Charley, but the voice on the phone announced that this number was not receiving calls at this time. *A terrible time to have his phone turned off.* Davis, anxious to share this new information with his police friend, was sorely disappointed.

"I'm elated you came out of yesterday's ordeal with no more than a few scratches," Ted told Deidre while they sat around her kitchen table with coffee cup in hand. "I was really worried about you. You were obviously lucky. I hope the authorities catch those guys before they seriously hurt someone."

"I really don't think luck had a lot to do with it, Ted. I'm sure the Lord watched over me."

"I would like to believe that, but such an idea is rather contrary to where I find myself at the present time. Why didn't God watch over Mandy and little Jerry when they were killed by that drunk driver? As a matter of fact, where was God when my marriage turned sour? Maybe it will surprise you to know that Mandy and I were on the verge of divorce when she was killed, and God did not intervene then." Ted's apparent bitterness spewed out.

"I can't answer those questions for you, Ted," Deidre told him just before taking a sip of her coffee. "You know as well as I that we will never understand all the reasons God does or doesn't take certain actions in this life or why He allows one incident and not another. But we don't have to understand in order to trust Him. The one fact I do know is that God loves me more than anyone else loves me, and I know I can count on Him one hundred per cent of the time to do what is ultimately best for me."

"I wish I could have that kind of faith, but it's not that simple for me. All that was pretty much cut and dried back when we were in high school, and I guess I got along fairly well back then. Most of the guys and especially the girls liked me, even admired me a little bit I think, but it hasn't been easy for me as an adult. It's been hard to stay afloat over these last ten years or so. I feel I have never been able to measure up to what people expect of me." Ted scooped a spoonful of sugar which he stirred into his coffee.

"I suppose your family and friends have always had high expectations for you, but that is because you always seemed to have so much potential. When we were in high school you had the grades, the looks, and the personality—and I guess the family background. No wonder you were voted the 'most likely to succeed' by your classmates. You seemed to have it all. But Ted, I think you know there is only one person you are obligated to please, and that, of course, is God."

"That may be true, but I don't do a very good job of pleasing Him either. I think I am a big disappointment to God as well as everyone else. Deidre, there are some allegations that will come down in the next few days. Will you promise me that no matter what you hear about me, you will never turn against me?"

"Yes, I can promise you that. There are promises I could never make to you, but I can assure you that you will always be my friend and have my absolute, unconditional support. Let me encourage you to do something for me. Would you talk with Pastor John? I understand you do not know him well, but I feel sure he can help you get on your feet again. Will you do that?"

"I don't know, Deidre. I'll think about it, but I don't know if anyone can help at this point."

It was always a special treat for Charley to have dinner with his older brother Dean and his family. It was especially good for him today since it enabled him to get his mind off what had happened to Deidre yesterday. Ambria, his niece, was still at home and a high school student. Dean and Sherry had two sons. Tommy was in college on a football scholarship down in Statesboro, while Evan recently began his hitch in the military. Tonight they would celebrate Charley's newly acquired pilot's license, which was really just an excuse to get together.

"We don't do this enough," Charley told his brother. "It's not hard to figure out why you have gained so much weight. Sherry has to be the best cook in town."

"I appreciate that compliment, but it's not true. I am no more than an average cook at best. It's just because you eat so much fast food that you are in awe of a real meal," Sherry said, seemingly to scold her brother-in-law. "You could have homecooked meals all the time if you would find a good girl and settle down."

"I love good homecooking, but I'm not sure I love it that much. Edible food is not a strong enough reason to tie myself down to one girl for the rest of my life."

"You don't know what you are missing," Dean insisted. "I couldn't function without my family. I highly recommend it. And understand it is more than beans and potatoes. Do you have any good prospects right now? I know you have gone out several times recently with that clerk out at the motel—what's her name?"

"I think you mean Debbi. She's a lot of fun, but I wouldn't want to spend the rest of my life with her. She has been helpful to me with a case—would you pass the salt?" Charley asked his niece.

"That's your problem," Sherry suggested, "You spend all your time with cases; even when you are off duty, you work."

"Let him alone," Ambria defended her uncle. "Everybody is different. Uncle Charley knows what he enjoys, and he has the right to do whatever he chooses without a lot of hassle. It's okay if he doesn't want to get married now or ever. Let him be himself."

"You're right, honey," Dean admitted to his daughter. "It's just that I love what I have so much I figure everyone should buy into it." He reached over to put his arm around the shoulder of his wife sitting next to him. "As for the police work, I guess he gets it from ole 'Chief'—our dad. He loved police work every bit as much as Charley and devoted his life to it. As for me, I would rather pull an engine any day. Charley, you know anytime you have had enough of chasing drunks I'm ready to make you a partner."

"I appreciate that, Dean, but I'm not anxious to go back to all that grease and twelve-hour days. I had plenty of that in the two years I worked with you before I got on the force. I may someday find a wife and settle down like an ordinary person if I can find the right girl," Charley explained. "But I'll not settle. She must be beautiful and have it all together, my kind of girl in every way."

"Good luck with that," Sherry remarked. "I'm not sure we have any unattached, perfect girls left in Adairsville since I married your brother."

"He got the cream of the crop all right, but I'm not interested in 'the perfect girl.' I'm after the one who is perfect for me, and I figure she is out there somewhere."

I wonder what she is doing right now and who she is with, was the thought that ran through Charley's mind.

"I just hope you do not set your sights too high," Sherry told him. "There are lots of good girls around, and I would be happy to introduce you to some of them."

"My love life is one matter I would rather handle myself," Charley laughingly told his sister-in-law.

"Wise move, Brother," Dean spoke up. "Have you met any of her unmarried friends?"

Davis once again tried to reach Charley, this time while the policeman drove back to his apartment after his dinner with his brother. "Hello, Davis," Charley said when he looked at the number on the screen of his cell. "What's on your mind?"

"You are a hard fellow to reach. I've tried to get hold of you several times today. A cell phone isn't of much use if you don't keep it turned on."

"A man has to have a little time to himself," Charley informed his friend. "What is it that is so important you've got to talk with me this very moment?"

"I found some information that might help you. While I looked through some of Miss Helen's columns, I found one in which she says there was a large group of former Confederate soldiers and their families from our area who settled in Santa Barbara, Brazil, after the Civil war. I'm sure you remember that was the home of our tattooed man."

"Yes, but why is that so important? The Civil War ended when? Maybe a hundred and fifty years ago."

"If that was all I found, like you I would probably conclude that a Santa Barbara citizen in Adairsville was of no real importance. But there is more. Miss Helen states that the name of one of the families that went to that city after the Civil War was 'Norris,' the name of our corpse with a set of directions tattooed on his chest, in Cherokee no less."

"I guess that could mean something, but it may mean that Norris was here to simply research his roots when he happened to have a heart attack."

"I thought about that, but how do you explain the directions on his body? That would seem to indicate that he was here for more than to gather facts about his genealogy."

"You may be right. I need to think about it for a while. How's Deidre doing after her ordeal yesterday?

"You know Deidre, always brave and ready to move on, but I think it affected her more than she is letting on. We need to watch her closely."

"I agree. She needs you right now. Stay close. Hey, its official—I got my pilot's license today. Are you ready to fly with me?"

"Whenever you want," Davis informed him. "You arrange for the plane and let me know when and where and I will be there."

"You better not get cold feet," Charley warned him. "If you back out, I'll tell Dean and the boys about that yellow streak, and you will never live it down."

"Not only am I not afraid, but I look forward to it. I love to fly," Davis stretched the truth just a little since he loved to fly commercially, but had little interest in riding in a small private craft.

"But you have never flown with me as your pilot," Charley reminded him before there was dead air on the line.

I've got to teach that boy some telephone etiquette, Davis told himself before he put his phone back into his pocket.

CHAPTER 11

After he read Miss Helen's article on the Confederate defection to Brazil, Davis knew he had to speak to Miss Helen again. Since she didn't hear well, the telephone was not a good option for an interview. So here he was on a late Wednesday morning, again in Miss Helen's parlor drinking a glass of her sweet tea and forced to endure her tongue-lashing about his defection from the ministry. He was finally able to break into the conversation after he listened for several minutes to her strong admonition about the ministry being a calling only the Lord could take back.

"Miss Helen, I need to ask you some questions about one of the articles you wrote." Davis used the voice he usually reserved for outside so as not to be required to repeat the statements and questions over and over.

"I am more than happy to answer any question I can about what I've written. Which column can I help you with?"

"It's the one you did about the people who resettled in Brazil after the Civil War. You mentioned that the Norris family was among those to go there. Can you tell me about them?"

Miss Helen went into a trancelike silence obviously to allow her mind to ponder the question. After a couple of minutes, she spoke to her inquisitive guest. "You understand that what I can tell you about that is second- or third-hand information? You do know that even though I am an old lady, I was not around when the Civil War ended?"

"I had a pretty good idea that was the case," Davis said, laughing. "But while it is true you have lived for a lot of years, I don't consider you old at all. You are just very experienced—seasoned, some would say."

"Well, I thank you for that observation, but we both know I am as old as dirt. As to the Norris family, I remember very little other than that they were at one time extremely prominent in the area. It seems to me that Mama told me that Mr. Norris's name was James. Yes," she said with her hand on her chin, "it was James, and I believe his wife was Claire and they had several children. I think she originally came from the mountains east of here, and I remember there was some kind of controversy about her that may have been a factor in why they choose to leave Adairsville for Brazil. I am sorry I can't remember what the dispute was about, but it was definitely a controversy of some kind that revolved around Claire."

"Can you think of any other details about the family?"

"From what I heard, James was a good soldier, highly respected by the veterans with whom he served. I think he spent some time in a Yankee prison. I believe he was still a rather young man when they pulled up roots and went to Brazil."

"As usual, you have been very helpful, Miss Helen, and I appreciate it." Davis knew that sometimes after Miss Helen had time to meditate on matters, she remembered more clearly, so he added, "If you come up with more information about the Norris family, please let me know."

Davis laughed to himself when he left Miss Helen's house with the thought, *I always feel like Daniel who escaped the lion's den or Jonah who was vomited out of the belly of the big fish when I make my escape from Miss Helen. I think I am either going to have to go back to ministry or spend less time with Miss Helen. She is one determined lady.*

Business was slow in the bookshop. *It would hardly have been worth my presence here today but for that one good sale,* Davis decided.

But he knew that was the way of the book business. It is possible to go for several days with little business, and then suddenly make one sale that would justify a week's effort. The purchase earlier that day would not give him a good week's income, but the three signed Eugenia Price books and two Celestine Sibley mysteries that the collector bought would certainly help.

"How's the book business?"

Davis looked up to see Kerry Austin, Jay and Amy's realtor, enter the shop with a broad smile on his face.

"Probably not as good as the real estate business," Davis speculated. "But I haven't missed many meals and am able to pay most of my bills."

"In today's economy, that is about as much as you can hope for. I haven't sold a house in a while. That's why I look forward to Jay and Amy's appointment tomorrow. Not only will we make them happy, but I will also put a little grocery money in my pocket."

"I know they are anxious to make it official so they can start work on the house. With all the work that will come with it I don't know if it is a wise move for them, but that is their business, and they are excited about it. As Amy's father, I appreciate your part in making their dream come true."

"That's my job," the realtor informed him. "I know you are interested in Reed Johnson, the North Carolina businessman who tried to purchase the Ammon property. He called me earlier today to see if the sale is still on, and I, of course, informed him that it was, which did not make him a happy camper. He told me if Jay backed out, he wanted to immediately make the purchase. When I asked him why he was interested in that particular piece of ground, he informed me he was a businessman who wanted to make an investment. Then I suggested to him that I have other property listed that would be a better investment and he cursed and told me he was only interested in the Ammon property."

"Did you get any more personal information about him?"

"Not really. He seemed to deliberately withhold information about himself. He did ask if I thought Jay and Amy might want to keep the house with a couple of acres and sell him the remainder of the land. I told him he could talk with them about that, but I doubt they would want to do that since one of the reasons they liked this property was that it gave them room to have some horses."

"How did he respond to that?" Davis asked.

"Again, he was unhappy and muttered some unintelligible comments about people and their animals before he abruptly hung up."

"Thank you for the information, Kerry. Mr. Johnson doesn't seem like a very pleasant person to deal with."

"No, he isn't, but as you know, in business you meet all kinds. Will you attend the closing with Jay and Amy tomorrow?" Kerry asked his friend.

"No, a young man doesn't need his future father-in-law tagging along when he handles these important matters. He and Amy should be allowed to proceed with this all by themselves. They are adults. They don't need my help."

"You are a considerate man, Davis. I hope you have a great afternoon," Kerry told him as he walked toward the front door.

Davis sat down to consider what Kerry had just told him, which left him a little concerned. *For some unknown reason, Johnson is determined to have that property and seems to be ready to go to just about any extent to get it. Maybe I need to go out there and walk the property to see if I can determine what he is after.*

Because he didn't want to run the risk of being late for his dinner with Deidre, Davis left the shop shortly after three o'clock to drive out to Folsom. He pulled into the driveway at the Ammon house and stopped for a moment to take a close look at the structure.

Oh, my! he thought, *I had forgotten how-run down it is. Jay and Amy have their work cut out for them.*

He let the engine run while he got out to walk up the steps onto the porch to look through a couple of windows. Again, he was not encouraged by what he saw, but his favorite couple had thoroughly looked it over and hired an inspector to give them a report. They had approached it eyes wide open.

One of the great advantages of a Jeep is that you can take it just about anywhere. Since Miss Helen recalled that the cave was about a half mile directly behind the house, Davis steered his Wrangler in that direction, careful to stay on the upper side of the hill where it was dry so as not to end up in a deep mud hole that even a four-wheel drive Jeep could not maneuver. Davis stopped his vehicle when he came to a spot approximately a half mile from the house where there were a lot of huge rocks visible on top of the ground. As a result of his teen exploration experience, he knew this was the kind of place where caves were usually found.

Davis observantly walked around the area and found no cave, though there was certainly the possibility that one could have been sealed shut here. One of the guys at breakfast had remarked that the Ammon cave had been sealed a few years back. If that were indeed the case, then this was most likely the spot. Davis estimated that the place where he stood was probably on the property that Jay and Amy would purchase, with the property line most likely a few hundred feet to the south.

A short distance from where he parked, in a grove of pine trees, he saw that someone had left empty tin cans, discarded food packages and other trash, even a small trash bag presumably filled with household type trash. He also noticed tire tracks, some of them small such as those that might be mounted on a camper. He recalled Deidre's account of Stringbean and the Sumo Wrestler with a camper. Davis wondered if perhaps this could have, for a time, been their campsite. That certainly would explain why Charley had found no evidence of them at any of the Adairsville motels. *Boy, would I like to get my hands on them.*

After he returned to the Jeep, Davis looked at his watch and decided he needed to get back home in time to shower and change clothes before he and Deidre would go to the Adairsville Inn for dinner.

Two men watched from the pine trees and bushes on a hillside.

"That's the kid's soon-to-be father-in-law," the tall skinny one remarked. "He is the guy who walked in on us at the motel when we were taking care of business. It looks like he found our old campsite."

"It doesn't matter," the short stocky one with the buzz haircut responded. "He can't hurt us. He's probably just interested in the property his little girl intends to buy. If they are like most newlyweds these days, it is probably Daddy who hands out the money, and I guess it is only natural that he wants to know what he has gotten."

"Well, we've got only until two o'clock tomorrow afternoon to stop that sale or we don't get the best payday we've had in a while," the tall man moaned.

"We'll get it done. I've got an idea that can't help but work."

"Yeah, you said that before, but none of your ideas have worked yet, and we're almost out of time."

"This one will work. A dead man can't buy a house," he told his tall partner.

Despite how Davis felt about Deidre, he still had guilt when he was with her in a situation that seemed more like a date than just two friends getting together for dinner. Perhaps it was the age difference or the fact that he still felt married to Julie even after she had been with the Lord now for some time. For whatever reason, a date with Deidre seemed inappropriate for him, while at the same time he relished every moment he had with the beautiful and personable young history teacher.

"Charley assured me he would keep a close eye on Amy, Barbara, and Jay while we are here tonight," Davis told his dinner companion when they were seated at one of the smaller tables at the Adairsville Inn. "I worry that those two guys who abducted you will come back to somehow try to shipwreck tomorrow's property closing or worse. They seem to be determined to stop it, and they have only until tomorrow at two o'clock to get that done."

"I wouldn't worry too much about them," Deidre added. "They are scary, but I am not sure those two are competent enough to stop a forty-year-old crippled dog. They probably haven't found their way back from Plainville yet."

"I know they are not very sharp, but sometimes that can be the real problem. You never know what illogical stunt such ineptness might lead to. But let's not spend our time talking about those bozos. Let's enjoy our dinner."

After the waitress had taken their order, Deidre remarked that Ted had borrowed Jay's car for a trip to Cartersville. "I'm really worried about him," she told Davis. "He is dangerously down on life, and there is some news about to come to light that is really weighing heavy on his mind."

"You like him a lot, don't you?" Davis said, smiling at the beautiful lady across the table.

Deidre looked at him questioningly, and he hoped he hadn't betrayed his mild case of jealousy.

"He has been my friend for much of my life. I was probably about ten or eleven years old when his Dad became our preacher and they moved to town. We also lived just a few houses apart, so we were playmates along with about five or six other kids in the neighborhood. We were in youth group together at church and were in the same school, even though he was a grade ahead of me. He went off to college the year before I graduated, and I have seen very little of him since. I think you know that his wife and young son were killed by a drunken driver a few years back."

"Yes, I was aware of that. That must have been a real blow to him. You mentioned his present outlook on life. Perhaps he has never gotten over that catastrophe."

"I am sure that is a factor in his current condition. I won't go into detail, but I think he feels some guilt over what happened to his wife and child, but it is more than that. Somewhere along the line he has gotten off track with the Lord. That has caused him to try to cope with the expectations of life with only his own power and ability."

"If that is the case, it is easy to see why he struggles. None of us are strong enough to do that."

"I suggested to him that Pastor John might be able to help him, but as far as I know he has not taken any strides to make that happen."

Davis enjoyed the roast beef, mashed potatoes, and green beans immensely, but more than that, he enjoyed his time with the lovely lady who had become such an important part of his life. He never ceased to be amazed at how easy it was to spend time with her. Conversation was never strained, and even the moments of silence produced no awkwardness. He realized that he felt more at ease with Deidre than any woman he had ever known with the exception of Julie who had been his companion and sweetheart for almost twenty-five years. When cancer took her, Davis thought there would never be anyone else who could step in to take that spot in his life, but now he wondered if perhaps the Lord had sent this wonderful young woman his way for a reason.

"You do remember that you promised me a trip to Gibbs Gardens before school starts, don't you?" Deidre's sweet voice broke into his thoughts. "We don't have long left to fit it in."

"What about next Thursday?" Davis suggested. "The wedding will be over, the house will have been purchased, and we will be free to do whatever we please."

"It's a date," Deidre smiled before she took a sip of her water.

Davis immediately wished she had not used that word. For some reason it brought him down.

The cell phone in Davis's pocket rang. "I am sorry, but I suppose I ought to take this. It's Amy," he said when he looked at the number displayed on the screen. "Hello, Amy." Davis was silent as he listened to his daughter. "We will be there in a moment," he responded in a tone of urgency. He stood to put his phone back into his pocket. Davis looked at Deidre with a long face before he told her, "Ted has been shot!"

CHAPTER 12

When Davis pulled to a halt in front of the little house on College Street, there was already a police car and an ambulance parked in the driveway of Jay and Amy's soon-to-be temporary home. Barbara walked beside the gurney on which her son lay. Two uniformed attendants, one at the front and one at the back, manned the stretcher. Deidre immediately ran to Barbara. She smiled and her face relaxed when Ted lifted his head to greet her.

"You people in Adairsville play rough," he jested.

"I can't tell you how good it is to hear your voice," Deidre said to her friend.

"If this is what it takes to get your attention, then I guess it's worth it," Ted told her with a slight smile as the attendants put him into the emergency vehicle.

"I'll ride with Barbara to the hospital," Deidre called back to Davis.

"I'll meet you there," Davis responded before he made his way to where Charley and Rayford, another young policeman, were in conversation.

"What happened here, Charley?" Davis inquired.

"It looks like someone took a shot at him from over there as he got out of the car." Charley pointed to the other side of the street. Obviously whoever did it was not a very good shot. My best guess is he aimed for the heart, but got him above that, in the shoulder. Isn't that Jay's Ford?" Charley asked.

"Yes, it is. Ted borrowed it to make a trip to Cartersville. As you know, Ted came to Adairsville as the driver of the van his mother rented, so he is without transportation here."

"Do you have any idea why he went to Cartersville tonight?" Raymond asked.

"No, I don't really know, but I am sure his mother could tell you or perhaps Jay. He has been Jay's guest since he came to town, and they have gotten to be friends. How badly is Ted hurt?" Davis asked.

"I'm not a doctor, but I think he will be fine. The rifle slug entered the front of his body and passed through, then exited out the back. The location of the wound leads me to believe no vital organs have been damaged. They will x-ray him at the hospital and treat his wound. I wouldn't be surprised if he is dismissed by sometime tomorrow."

"That's good news. I don't know Ted well, but he is a good friend of Deidre's. I would hate for him to be seriously injured here in our little town. I suspect his opinion of our hospitality is pretty low about now."

Charley walked toward those who were stringing yellow crime scene tape to give them needed instruction before he stuck his head in his patrol car to retrieve a pad on which he wrote down what Davis had told him.

Five minutes later, before he started to the Floyd Medical Center, Davis again sought out Charley and told him, "I don't know why this happened here tonight, but you know as well as I that it's another good reason to keep a close eye on Jay and Amy between now and tomorrow at two o'clock. There may be no connection whatsoever, but who knows?"

"Don't worry. That had already crossed my mind, and I will personally make sure Jay and Amy are closely guarded right through the closure tomorrow and beyond if needed."

"I knew I could count on you. A man couldn't have a better friend," Davis sincerely complimented him.

"Why should you worry when you have your personal policeman who constantly stands by to take care of your every whim?" Charley facetiously replied. "We will make sure they are not harmed," he said.

Davis took time to talk to the Lord while he drove the twenty-five miles to Rome. As a pastor Davis had sat with loved ones of a critical patient many times through the years, but had never found it easy to give the help he so desperately wanted to provide. Words never seemed to help much during those months when he was watching Julie slip away. He had long ago learned that the most effective action he could take was to simply be there and pray.

Upon his arrival in the trauma center, Deidre gave him a report that indicated Charley was pretty much on target with his evaluation of Ted's condition. "Unless the x-rays show an unexpected complication, they will keep him for the rest of the night and release him in the morning," Deidre told him.

Davis tried to occupy Barbara's mind as she waited with him and Deidre in the busy waiting area of the emergency room. She smiled at him when he rather awkwardly tried to assure her, and she tightly gripped his hand with both of hers when he offered it to her. He wondered if she was now regretting her decision to move to such a town. *Having your son shot by a sniper isn't a great way to say welcome to our town.*

When Barbara was finally permitted to go back to the treatment area to see Ted, Davis asked Deidre, "When you were kidnapped by those two goons the other day, did you see a rifle?"

"Why, yes I did. I noticed there were two rifles in a gun rack in the back of the cab of the truck. You don't think those two were behind this, do you?"

"I don't know. It's hard to say, especially since you learned that Ted was expecting bad news, but think about it. Ted got out of Jay's car. He is about the same build with the same color of hair, and he was in the drive at the place where Jay currently lives, and it all happened in the dark. Doesn't it make sense that the inept Sringbean and Sumo Wrestler could have thought they shot Jay?"

"You're right. When you look at the facts, it makes all the sense in the world. Did you tell that theory to Charley?" Deidre quickly asked.

"Yes, he understands there could be that connection, but we don't need to jump to any conclusions. It could very well be that the sniper was actually gunning for Ted or it could be random."

Despite the objections from her son, Barbara decided to spend the rest of the night at the hospital. Deidre told her she would come by tomorrow and drive them back to Adairsville. On the way home the couple discussed the strange events over the past few days and decided they would welcome a little less excitement, but in the midst of all that had happened, God's protection had been evident. "Like a shield," Deidre suggested.

It was shortly after daybreak when the cell phone on the small table between the camper bunks rang. Both the tall man and the short stout one rose up at the sound, but it was the short one who took the call.

"Hello boss, you are up early today. The sun is hardly up yet."

"Just an early reminder that you had better get with it. You have until two o'clock today to complete your assignment and just in case you don't remember, if you don't get the job done, there will be no payday."

"I'm pretty sure we took care of that last night. I plugged the kid. I don't know if he is dead, but I do know he will be in no condition to sign any papers today. I suspect that will scare them away for good."

"You incompetent fool! Can't you get anything right? You didn't shoot the kid; you brought down the wrong guy."

"That's impossible. It was the kid's car, at his house, and it looked exactly like him. How could it be the wrong guy?"

"I don't know, but it was. You've got one more chance, and you had better get it right this time. There is a lot of money riding on this."

"Don't worry, boss, we'll find a way. Believe me, he will not show up for that appointment with the realtor today."

"Why should I believe you? So far you have kidnapped the wrong girl and shot the wrong guy. No, I have no reason to worry, no reason at all," he sarcastically stated. "Just remember that I have a lot at stake on this deal, and if the job is not completed, there will be no money. That is one fact on which you can count. Don't mess it up again!"

Amy rose early, her mind torn between all the weird things happening and the reality of the wonderful dreams about to be fulfilled. She could not believe that before the day was over she would have her own home, even though it would be several months before she would be able to move in. Her dad had hinted that she and Jay should rethink that purchase, but the plan was still to sign the papers to buy the house today and get married Saturday. Despite the problems, she and Jay decided they would move forward as planned. *I wish Mom where here to experience it all with me. She was always so thrilled for me when life was going my way. I think she was happiest when I was happy. I miss her so very much.*

Caught up in her thoughts while she put the bread in the toaster, Amy did not hear Deidre enter the kitchen. "You're up early today," Deidre said, smiling at her friend.

"It's a big day for me, and I guess the anticipation was too much. I decided I might as well get up. I have never much liked to stay in bed to wait for the sun to come up so I could rise. You're up rather early yourself. You better take advantage of these last days of summer vacation."

"You're right; it will be back to work soon. Just a couple of weeks till school is back in session and there will be few chances to sleep in then. I guess I ought to take advantage of the opportunity, but I just can't get all that happened last night and over the past few days off my mind."

"Have you heard from Barbara and Ted yet?"

"No, not yet, but Barbara will call sometime before the morning is over. I told her I would drive over to pick them up when Ted is discharged."

"I know you and Ted were sweethearts long ago, so do you think that romance could be rekindled?" Amy's curiosity had gotten the better of her, so she just blurted out the question.

"We were just kids who had a crush on one another. It was never really a romance, and the answer to your question is no. Ted is a friend and I like him a lot, but there can never be a strong romantic relationship in our future. And besides, I think you know there is someone else who has captured my heart."

"Do you mean Dad?" Amy stopped buttering her toast and looked directly at Deidre.

"Yes, I do. I don't know that he has any real romantic interest in me, but I sure hope and pray that he does, because I think I love him."

"Oh, Deidre, you cannot imagine how thrilled I am!" Amy declared as she embraced her friend while tears formed in her eyes. "I too have been hopeful and have often prayed for this for several weeks now. I know that Dad feels the same way about you. I have never heard him speak of another woman other than Mom with such admiration as when he talks of you. And he has that same light in his eyes when he looks at you as he had when he looked at Mom. You two are perfect for one another."

"I don't know that we are *perfect* for one another, but I do know that I care a lot for him, and I understand that love can overcome a lot of obstacles. I guess one of the anticipated roadblocks really wasn't a problem at all. I didn't know how you would feel about me and your Dad as a couple. I thought it would be hard for you to accept your roommate who is much closer to your own age than your father's age as a companion for him."

"I've never had any such thoughts. Should this go as I hope it does, it is true that I would never think of you as a mother. You will always be my big sister, but I assure you it would never be a problem for me to accept you as my dad's wife."

"Well, I am delighted to know that, but let's not go there yet. Your dad has never even kissed me other than on the cheek or forehead. He has never told me he loves me or given me any real indication that he is interested in a life commitment. We certainly have not yet reached the point where we need to reserve the church."

The two young ladies, one who anticipated her own wedding in three days and the other with so many hopes and dreams, sat down at the table to eat their toast and drink coffee. They talked and laughed for at least an hour before they got up to start the activities of the day, with no knowledge of what that day would bring.

CHAPTER 13

It was Thursday, the day scheduled for Jay and Amy's official closing. Davis paced the floor in his living room, occasionally stopping to be seated and then getting up to start the pacing all over again. In light of the events of the past few days, they could expect some kind of resistance before the two o'clock hour. In the peacefulness of predawn, it was hard to believe that such evil was present around him. It was difficult to perceive that people with guns were out there trying to hurt the innocent in order to get what they wanted. But it is real, he told himself, and we would be foolish to ignore it. Davis recalled the Biblical instructions that had so often been his guide in difficult times,

"Be on your guard; stand firm in the faith; be men of courage; be strong. Do everything in love. (I Corinthians 16:13)

He decided he would accept that as his assignment for this day.

Davis looked out one of the windows in the front room to observe the police car that had sat in his driveway when he peeked out the same window three hours earlier had been moved to the lot next door. *Charley kept his promise. A guard was posted.* After he had a light breakfast, a shower and dressed for the day, Davis sat down in his favorite chair with some of Miss Helen's columns. He would stay as close to Amy and

Deidre as possible. Janie could take care of business at the shop today. But he soon found that he could not concentrate on what he was doing. He laid aside his work to silently reflect over the last twenty-three years. It seemed like yesterday when Amy came into the world two days before Christmas, a beautiful seven-pound baby with dark hair that later almost disappeared to grow back much lighter than before.

From the time she could walk, Amy brought great liveliness to his and Julie's lives. Her curiosity had always been unquenchable, which created the need to watch her constantly. How many times had they pulled her out of some potentially dangerous situation to which her inquiring mind had led her? Julie said a number of times that Amy's guardian angel had to be devoted because of the amount of overtime he had to work. Here it was again, after all those years. She still needed to be closely guarded in order to remain safe. He hoped her guardian angel was still on duty. He was certainly needed.

With his thoughts centered on Amy, Davis at first thought the sound of her voice came out of his own mind. "Dad, how did you sleep last night?" His only daughter stood before him as radiant and beautiful as he had ever seen her. It wasn't the makeup that she wore, because it was obvious she had not yet taken care of that daily chore. The beauty he saw was not the result of some fantastic outfit she had chosen. She wore faded jeans and a ragged football jersey. Her hair, chopped short, was the same as it had been for the last couple of years. Then what was it that made her such a gorgeous figure as she stood before him today? Could it be that he really saw her for the first time? No, it was more than that, and her next move enabled him to get a handle on exactly what it was.

"Dad, I am so happy!" Amy said in the sweetest of all voices when she sat down on the arm of his chair. She put her arms around his neck and her head on his shoulder to hug him tightly. Tears formed in his eyes and he fought hard to keep them from flowing down his cheeks. The father at that moment understood that the beauty he observed before him was the overflow of pure happiness!

Being too choked up to speak, Davis thought, *What a girl! No, what a woman! Here she is in the midst of all kinds of potential danger and she's the happiest person alive. That's my Amy!*

The two, father and daughter, stayed in that position for three or four minutes. She sat on the arm of the chair with her arms tightly around her father's neck, and he reached up to put his right arm around his daughter. Amy's shoulder was digging into his neck and it hurt, but there was nothing in this world that would cause him to let go. It was for Davis the most comfortable position in which he had ever found himself.

The excitement started at a roadblock on the corner of College and Railroad Street, one of four such roadblocks. With a persistent effort, Charley had convinced Chief Hanson to carry out the plan. It was in place at about nine thirty the previous night. No one was able to pass Davis's house, where Amy was, or the little house on College Street, where Jay had spent the night without being checked out by an Adairsville policeman. From the time the roadblocks were set up until mid-morning the officers had stopped and questioned a number of people in white pickup trucks, but until now none of them had proven to be the two strange, bad guys.

When Raymond, the newest of the officers, motioned for the tall driver to pull over, he stomped the accelerator and turned the truck around with tires squealing. Raymond got a quick look at the short man on the passenger side. These two fit the description of the men they were after. Before he stomped the accelerator to pull behind the truck which now turned left on George Street, Raymond put out a call with the appropriate information, "Spotted suspects headed west on George Street."

Charley was parked next door to the house on Railroad Street when he heard the call and immediately started in that direction. It took him only seconds to catch Raymond who was now on the tail of the two fugitives. They passed the elementary school which fortunately was not in session. The truck with the two suspects crossed Hall Station Road where it became Twin Bridges Road without stopping, with Raymond right behind them. Charley with his siren on and lights flashing turned right onto Hall Station and then left on Highway 140 at a speed as fast as safety would allow. As a lifetime resident of the town, Charley knew that Twin Bridges intersected 140. If he could get there ahead of the white pickup, he could stop them there.

The truck, which consistently gained speed, went into a skid at the curve near the Adairsville water works, but managed to stay on the road. Raymond, less than a hundred feet behind them, saw the short passenger reach to the gun rack in the back of the cab for a rifle. He knew he would be an easy target, so the young policeman backed off a bit, but continued to stay close enough to keep them in sight.

The culprits had a shorter distance to travel to the intersection than Charley, but he knew he had the better road. The race would be close. He understood it probably wasn't a wise move, but he gave it just a little more gas. He so wanted to apprehend these guys that he went a little beyond caution. When he approached the intersection, he did not see the white truck.

They had gotten ahead of him and were now well down the road or he had gotten there before them. He assumed the latter was true and turned his vehicle onto Twin Bridges Road. Then he backed it cross the road in order to block the way of the fugitives. He had no sooner gotten out of the car than he saw the white truck cannon balling toward the car blocking its way.

Charley pulled his gun from his holster even before dropping into place in a ditch beside the road. Then when he saw the speed of their approach, he panicked. *Those fools aren't going to stop.* There was a loud sound of metal crashing into metal when the pickup plowed headlong into his patrol car. The two vehicles seemed almost to weld together as the cruiser wrapped itself around the front of the truck. Both of the crushed vehicles were now sitting in the middle of Highway 140.

By this time Raymond brought his patrol car to a halt and opened the door to get out. Charley yelled to him, "Raymond, call 911!" In light of what he saw, he was glad the fire station with the emergency vehicles and EMTs was located only a couple of minutes away. Both Charley and Raymond ran toward the wrecked vehicles with guns drawn. They hoped to reach the two men in the demolished truck before it burst into flames.

"It's hard to believe," Charley told Davis when they talked on the telephone. "My patrol car is totally destroyed and their truck isn't much better off, but neither one of them have any really serious injuries. They're banged up pretty good, and the tall one who was behind the wheel may have a broken rib or two, but they came out of it in remarkably good shape. The short one scrambled to find his gun and when he couldn't find it, tried to run, but Raymond didn't let him get too far. They were taken to the hospital for treatment; however, I don't think it will be long before they will be safely behind bars. You won't have to worry about them anymore."

"You can't imagine what a load that takes off my mind. Thank you, Charley, for a job well done. I know there is at least one more bad guy to identify and apprehend before this whole affair can be put to rest, but at least I feel like Amy and Jay will be safe when they go to that lawyer's office in a couple of hours. What did the chief have to say about your patrol car?"

"He hasn't actually seen it yet, but he knows that it is totaled. He isn't happy, but I'm sure he is glad those two were caught. He will forgive me in time I suppose."

"In the meantime, he may put you on a bicycle or maybe you will walk a beat," Davis suggested.

"I hope I will be assigned our spare vehicle until mine is replaced, but you could be right."

"Have a good day," the young policeman said before there was dead air.

Well, I guess his telephone manners have improved a bit. That was almost a goodbye. He's almost there and I hope that includes more than his telephone etiquette.

The contracts were signed three hours earlier and now it was official. The six people were at Deidre's apartment happily celebrating. Deidre earlier in the day picked Ted and his mother up from the Floyd County Medical Center. The two joined with Jay and Amy along with Davis and, of course, the hostess for this special dinner. The legal documents had been completed earlier, and Stringbean and the Sumo Wrestler were behind bars. Even Ted with his left arm in a sling seemed to be more upbeat than usual. Barbara appeared to be the most subdued of the group, with her mind at times seemingly somewhere else.

After dinner Ted turned to Deidre and asked, "Could we go sit on the front porch for a few minutes? There are some things I want to tell you."

Davis noticed Deidre's uncertain demeanor about how to respond to her friend's suggestion. "Why don't you two go have your talk in privacy while I take care of the dishes?" He hated doing dishes and he disliked Deidre and Ted spending time together, but he felt the right thing to do was to offer.

Deidre hesitated, but then agreed to go along with Ted's request. "I guess we can do that for a few minutes," she told him.

Amy and Barbara joined Davis to clean up the table while Jay was politely told to stay out of the way.

"I want to thank you for your kindness. Mom will take me to the Atlanta Airport to fly back to Savannah early Saturday morning," Ted stated while he looked down at the floor of the porch after they were seated in porch chairs. "I don't think it will be a problem for her to get back in time for Jay and Amy's wedding. I don't want her to miss that. Before I go, it is important to me that you know what I've been doing over the past two or three years."

"You don't have to tell me anything," Deidre quickly responded. "I'm glad to listen to what you feel you have to share, but understand you owe me no explanation." She took a sip of the iced tea she had brought with her to the porch.

"In a way I think I do. Even though we have seen very little of each other in recent years, there was a time when you were my best friend, and I would like very much to restore that friendship. Oh, it's not about romance. I know that is not in the cards, but it would mean a lot to me if I could know you are my friend."

"That is also what I want, Ted. I think you have probably realized I am in love with someone else, but that certainly doesn't take away my desire or ability to be your friend. I am sure Davis would also like to be your friend."

"I hope that will continue to be true after I tell you about my craziness over these past months." Ted got up from his chair to walk the three or four steps to where he placed both hands on the banister and looked out over the yard toward the railroad tracks. After a moment he spoke again. "I borrowed Jay's car yesterday to meet a friend of my dad who was also my boss for a short period of time. Jim is an extremely successful businessman who has his own plane. He stopped over at the Cartersville airport on his way to Lexington, Kentucky, so we could talk. I worked for him only about five months before I took the job I now have. I thought it would be good to get a taste of private business to see if maybe I could tolerate it better than I do the banking industry. I'm sure Jim offered me the job because of how he felt about my father. He was a deacon in the last church Dad served. To make a long story short, I took a good deal of money from him which was recently discovered by his accountants."

"Why would you do that, Ted? You are obviously a successful banker who makes a reasonable salary, a young man on his way up in his profession. Why would you need to steal?"

Ted returned to his chair and was again seated. "I guess I have grown accustomed to a lifestyle I can't afford, but the worst of it is that somewhere along the line I became addicted to a vice that drained me of most of my resources as well as money I didn't even have. I became a gambler. It started when I went into casinos while traveling on business, and it grew from there until I stole money with which to gamble in a futile effort to recoup what I had lost. I just got in deeper and there was no place to stop. It was the proverbial vicious circle. The problem continued to get worse until I was trapped. If Dad were alive, he would tell me, 'trapped by the Devil,' and he probably would be right. I haven't stolen from any of the banks for which I worked. The built-in checks and balances in that business make that next to impossible, but I owe Jim a substantial amount."

"So what now, Ted? Where does it go from here?"

"I have received a reprieve of sorts for which I will forever be grateful. Because of Jim's love for my father and I suppose because he is a Christian gentleman, he offered me some alternatives to prosecution. I must pay all that I owe him in the next three months." Ted again got out of his chair to turn away from Deidre.

"Is that possible? Can you do that?" Deidre asked.

"It won't be easy, but I think I will be able to get it done. I have a sports car that is still worth over thirty thousand dollars. I can probably get twenty or twenty-five thousand for it immediately, but taking the loss is okay if it keeps me out of prison. I have built up a good deal of equity in my house which I am sure a friend of mine will buy at a cut-rate price as an investment. That means I will have to live in a small rented apartment, but since I have no family, that is not a problem. I guess I am lucky to have valuables to sell even if I will be forced to let them go for less than their worth."

"It sounds to me like you are a blessed man, Ted. Jim is obviously the real deal. It takes a genuine relationship with the Lord to practice that kind of forgiveness. You should be thankful for such a friend."

"I am indeed thankful, but there is more. He insisted I become part of the Gambler's Anonymous program and regularly report to him my activity with that organization. Another condition he placed on me was that I would no longer work in a position where I must handle money. That, of course, means I will have to leave the banking business. He assured me he will help me find an appropriate job, but with no promises about the type of work or the amount of salary I will receive."

"Sounds like he has covered all the bases. How do you feel about those stipulations?"

There was a couple of minutes of silence as Ted again took his seat beside Deidre. "I am naturally a bit scared, but on the other hand you would not believe how relieved I am. In recent weeks I have actually contemplated suicide, but now that I have a second chance, I am determined I will not blow it!"

"I hope you mean that, Ted, but, as I am sure you know, there is only one sure way to keep that commitment, and that is to put yourself in the Lord's hands. I don't have to tell you that He can do through us what we cannot do for ourselves."

"I am well on my way to relearning that, Deidre. I told Mom the whole story at the hospital last night. She was hurt and came down on me pretty hard. We cried a lot and at her insistence we prayed together. I understand that all of this happened because I lost my way."

"I am thankful you have come to your senses," Deidre told her friend. "The journey ahead won't be easy, but you and the Lord can make it. I know that because I know you, but most of all because I know what the Lord can do."

The two friends talked for a while longer before they rejoined those inside who had by then finished the dishes and clean up. It was a good evening at the big white house on Railroad Street, a time when the air had been cleared for at least one and there was more to come.

CHAPTER 14

With his troubles with Stringbean and Sumo obviously behind him, Davis woke up in a good mood with a desire for a real breakfast. He decided to join the guys at the Little Rock on this Friday morning. It was the day before his daughter's wedding and he felt the need for human companionship. On his way to the café, Davis decided, *A person has to be really hard up to turn to these guys to satisfy his need for company. I've got to get out more.* Dean was already at the big round table which had pretty much become the morning property of the boisterous group of friends.

"Well, I know it is bound to be a special day when *the Reverend* shows up to bless us with his presence." Dean used the word 'reverend' in reference to Davis because he had learned it irritated the one-time pastor. Davis, though he never made an issue of the matter, believed the term, which means; worthy to be revered, belonged to the Lord Jesus. He had never cared too much for such titles. He preferred to be thought of as a minister, servant or even shepherd, but he knew that to make an issue of it with his friend would be to fall right into his trap.

"Sherry must have thrown you out of the house early today," Davis, who had finally learned to dish it out himself, retaliated.

"Tomorrow is the big day. Your little girl will become a wife. Are you ready for that to happen?"

"It doesn't make much difference whether or not I am ready. It will happen and I guess I have to accept it. Will you and Sherry be there for the ceremony and reception?"

"We'll be there with bells on, wouldn't miss it for the world."

"I'm glad we will be favored with your presence, but let me suggest you not wear bells. I'm not sure the world is ready for that."

"Are you guys ready to order or will you wait for the other clowns to join you?" It was Brenda, the only waitress in the establishment who could hold her own with the rowdy but fun group of friends.

"The others will be along shortly," Dean responded. "In fact, we may have a full table today. I believe Pete cleared his schedule in order to join us." Dean made reference to Pete Carson who was the proprietor of Pete's lumberyard and a contemporary of all the others.

"Wow, that ought to really increase your tip," Davis joked.

"Yeah, with six of you big spenders here, I probably can expect it to total almost a dollar."

"Speaking of money, Al is in the house," Dean reported as he pointed toward the banker when the door opened. "Red, Brad, and Pete are right behind him. I suppose you can take our orders now."

"All I need are the orders of the preacher and Pete. I gave the cook the others before I came out here."

"I will have an entirely different meal today," Dean said, laughing.

"And I have moved out of my crummy little apartment into that sixteen-room mansion I have always wanted," the poker-faced server retorted before she left and returned with a pot of coffee.

After all the six men were seated, the friends talked of the capture of the two kidnappers the previous day.

"They towed Charley's patrol car to the fenced area behind my garage," Dean told them. "I have dealt with wrecked cars for years, but I don't think I have ever seen one more totally totaled. There is no way anyone could have come out alive had that car been occupied. It is unbelievable the guys in the pickup made out as well as they did."

Brad stirred cream in his coffee before stating, "You can't hurt guys as mean as those two."

"Yeah, from what I hear they are about as dumb as they are mean," Red reported.

"Regardless of who or what they are, we won't have to worry about them for a few years. Those two old boys will do some time," Brad told his breakfast companions, "And I say good riddance. Guys like that don't need to be on the streets."

"Why were they so all fired determined to keep Jay and Amy out of that old house?" Al questioned Davis.

Davis sipped his coffee to find it a bit hotter than he liked before sitting it back on the table. "We don't really know. They haven't yet talked much, but I suspect they were hired to stop the purchase by someone who wants the property for himself."

"But what, all of a sudden, is so desirable about that old place?" Dean asked.

"I would sleep better if I knew the answer to that question," Davis replied.

"Do the police have any leads as to who is behind all the problems?" Al inquired.

"A couple of leads have turned up, but no solid clues yet," Davis told him. "But I think we will have some answers soon."

"Did you boys hear that?" Brad asked. "He said, *we*. Since they made him chaplain he thinks he is an officer. Where is your gun, Mr. Policeman? Will you shoot the criminals or pray for them?"

"I've prayed for you guys for years, but it doesn't seem to do a whole lot of good."

"Don't give up on us, Davis," Al suggested.

"Never," Davis said, grinning. "You guys may be rotten to the core, but you are my friends and I love you."

Davis's declaration of love seemed to quiet them down a bit. Conversation turned to political matters before Davis was bombarded by questions about the Saturday nuptials and the plans the couple had made for afterwards. Not knowing what outrageous prank to expect from this group, Davis was reluctant to give them too much information.

After breakfast, Davis went by the barbershop for a haircut. He usually got one about once a month. Only a little over half that time had elapsed since his last visit, but with the special event one day away, he decided it would be expedient to go ahead. He definitely did not want to be an embarrassment to his daughter.

There was one person in the chair when he got there and one other ahead of him. He picked up a sports magazine and read about three paragraphs of a baseball story before Sam Ellison came in and sat down beside him.

"Time for a haircut, Mr. Mayor?"

"You bet; I've got this big fancy wedding to go to tomorrow, and my wife insists I get a haircut," Ellison said, laughing. "The chief tells me we've got those two boys that have given you people so much trouble in lockup down in Cartersville. He told me that he hasn't been able to get much out of them so far. That doesn't mean he won't. They may be more apt to talk after they sit in those cells for a while."

"I am grateful the chief set up those road blocks. After Ted was shot, I knew it was just a matter of time before someone would get seriously hurt or worse if they were not caught."

"Give that boy Charley Nelson the credit. He is the one who came up with the idea and got the chief to implement it."

"He's a good cop, isn't he?"

"He's young and Chief Hanson tells me he's sometimes a little restless and impulsive, but he seems to have good instincts and, like his dad, he has a love for police work. If you tell him I spoke well of him, I will deny it."

"Don't worry; I am the last person who wants to give Charley a big head. He is hard enough to live with as it is."

Davis spent a couple of hours at his bookshop where he dusted, priced, and rearranged stock before he started home in mid-afternoon without even one book sold. "You will be at the big event tomorrow, won't you?" he asked of Janie on his way out.

"I'll be there with bells on," she responded.

"You are the second person today who told me they will be wearing bells. It must be a new trend."

The middle-aged man had anticipated this event for some time. There were a lot of important people present he had looked forward to meeting, but he could not keep his mind off that other matter. Everything had changed. The property had officially changed hands and it was not he who was the new owner.

His two employees were in the county jail and they could start singing at any time. *I think they know better, but I can't be sure. You can't be sure of anything with men like that. I knew I was making a mistake when I got tangled up with such washouts. I should have severed my ties with them when they botched the deal with that girl. Better still, I should never have gotten involved with them in the first place.*

He would now have to back up and start over again. He would find a way. There had to be a way. *I will not let this go. It's not over. Too much at stake.*

Since he had spent years in the ministry there had been many rehearsals in Davis's past, but this one was different. This was the first time he had been the father of the bride. Oh, how he wished Julie could be at his side throughout the festivities. The only danger would have been that she would have outshone the bride. But no, that would not have happened because she would not have allowed it. She would have made sure it was her daughter's day in every way. Amy was the apple of her eye. Mother and daughter had been inseparable. The agony Davis felt over Julie's absence from the wedding activities was almost enough to trigger the kind of bitterness and sadness he had experienced in the months immediately after she had passed, but he was determined that would not happen. It would not be fair to Amy, and at this moment there was no more important consideration than Amy's happiness.

Pastor John kept the rehearsal running smoothly. He first gathered all the wedding party together at the front of the church auditorium where he started with a prayer in which he asked the Lord to help them plan well.

After his prayer, he had all those who would be on the platform take their places. They walked through an abbreviated form of the ceremony before he led them to practice the recessional and then finally the processional. The whole process took only about forty-five minutes and everyone involved seemed to be confident that this brief walk-through was sufficient to ready them for the actual ceremony.

They traveled the three blocks down the hill to the Adairsville Inn for the rehearsal dinner. The festive minded group was, for the most part, made up of young people in the same age bracket as Jay and Amy. Davis was pleased by what he saw. These were well-behaved young adults who knew how to have a good time while they remained respectful of those around them. What he observed also reminded him again of the fact that he was no longer a young man. That was sometimes hard for him to swallow. Why did he think Deidre would be interested in a man so much older than her?

Davis's thoughts were interrupted by Deidre who sat to his right. "I think Amy looks just about as happy as I have ever seen her look."

"That is probably because she has never been happier. This is all fairy tale stuff for her. Her dream come true."

"And what about you, Davis? Are you also happy?" Deidre's question surprised Davis and he remained silent for a moment as he searched for an honest answer.

"At this point in life, my personal happiness is mostly tied to Amy's, so I guess you could say I'm happy. I miss her mother, but I am learning to live with that. Some very special people, present company included, have helped me cope with that void. I know I need to live my own life. After tomorrow Amy will have her own home with a husband and perhaps in the not so distant future her own children. I have got to work on rebuilding my own life, one that does not exclude her, but doesn't totally revolve around her either."

The dinner seemed to be a success, but Davis found himself going through the motions, so to speak, in a mild trance of sorts. He felt as if he were a minor character in someone else's dream. He was indeed happy for his only daughter, but a bit anxious about the changes this milestone in Amy's life would mean to his own.

The cell phone Davis carried was off throughout the rehearsal and the dinner. He turned it on after he escorted Deidre home to her side of the house. There was a message from Charley. "I trust all went well tonight and the knot can be permanently tied at the proper time tomorrow. I just wanted to tell you to look up when you come out of the church after the deed is done. Make sure that Amy and Jay do the same. Remember to look up!" Charley reemphasized before he abruptly concluded the call.

Look up! I wonder what that is all about. I guess it is Charley's way of telling me to keep my head up. It was a long bittersweet night for Davis. Sweet, as his mind reviewed the wonderful years of life with such an adorable daughter. There were so many unforgettable memories that flashed through his mind as he lay awake in his bed. Bitter because of his awareness that life doesn't remain exactly where we want it. First, Julie was gone; Julie, the woman who he expected to be his partner for life was no longer at his side to encourage him when he was down or to gently kick him a bit when he needed to be challenged. Julie, who was his sweetheart, his wife, his adviser and his lover was no longer in the picture and he missed her so.

The ministry had brought to him a real sense of satisfaction. It provided for him a sense of making a difference. Without Julie's companionship, a big part of what made it all work was gone. He just could not do it by himself.

And now Davis felt as if he had lost Amy. Oh, he understood she would continue to be close by and accessible, but their relationship would be different. He could certainly find some solace in her happiness, and the fact that it was all a part of life's natural progression. He was more than pleased with her choice of a husband. He knew she would always be treated appropriately and with love, but it was all this change that seemed to come upon him so rapidly that turned his world upside down. Such thoughts kept him awake until the wee hours of the morning.

CHAPTER 15

Before he got out of bed, Davis heard a car in the driveway. He knew it was Barbara on her way to get her son for the trip to the Atlanta Airport. He did not know the details of the young man's troubles, but he knew Ted was unhappy, so he took time to pray for him before he got out of bed.

Lord, you know better than I Ted's needs. I pray you would provide strength to enable him to make whatever adjustments he needs to make. Help him to remember what he has been taught through the years, that the best future for him lies in putting it all in Your hands and trusting You completely. May he not lean on his own strength, but realize that the best for him will be found in You. Be with his mother and enable her to release her son to Your care....

This was the day he had always known would come. He and Julie had often prayed about Amy's choice of a future husband long before she was even in preschool, and this was the day those prayers would come to fruition. The doubts he had experienced in the darkness and loneliness of the night had now given way to a guarded spirit of excitement and joy. Before this day was over his beautiful daughter would walk down that aisle to become Mrs. Jay Archer, and he was good with that. It was for her a dream come true, and for him, as her father, the fulfillment of twenty-plus years of prayer. How could it be other than a fantastic day?

Amy and her attendants would go to the church late morning to prepare for the two o'clock ceremony. Davis wanted to spend a moment with her on her special day, so he knocked on her apartment door. It was Deidre who answered the door and smiled at him before she took a step toward him to kiss his right cheek. "What was that for?" Davis asked with a big smile that said, *Regardless of the reason, I surely did enjoy it.*

"It was because you are a loving father and a special person," she told him before she embraced him with a hug. "I suppose you are here to see your daughter?"

"That is what I had in mind when I knocked on the door, but I sort of like what just happened," he said, laughing.

"She is in her bedroom; I'll go tell her you are here."

"Deidre!" Davis called to her when she started in the direction of Amy's room. "Thank you for being such a fantastic friend to Amy. She has told me again and again what you have meant to her over these past months. Thank you for your love and patience with her when she was mourning the loss of her mother and I was too much of a mess to help anyone, even my own daughter. You are one of God's most special creations and I am glad He sent you our way." Davis moved in the direction of the lovely woman with the angelic face and debated with himself, *Should I or shouldn't I?* Deep down he knew the answer, and he took her in his arms before he gave her a long tender kiss which she lovingly returned with her arms tightly wrapped around him. The wonderful scent of her perfume and the warmth of her lips were almost overwhelming.

"What's going on here?" Amy who had stepped into the room asked with a lighthearted tone to her voice. "I'm sure glad Barbara will be around to watch you two, otherwise I am not sure I could in good conscience leave you in the same house even separated by that big hallway and a locked door."

"It was just a friendly little kiss between two friends," Davis responded with a nervous laugh, embarrassed that his daughter caught him in such a position.

"It surely looked like more than that to me," Amy told her dad.

"And to me as well," Deidre said with delight in her voice. "If it was just a kiss between two friends, then why are my legs still weak and my head swimming?"

"Well, I guess I have to admit it was more than that, but I would rather talk about something else—anything else!" Davis told the two ladies before both of them broke into laughter.

Davis had his fifteen minutes with his daughter. "Honey, you know I love you and always will. There is absolutely no situation that could change that."

"There has never been a time when I doubted that for even one moment," Amy told her dad.

"Not even when you were thirteen and couldn't understand why I didn't buy you a horse, or when you were sixteen and I refused to give you that car you wanted?"

"Not even then," she emphatically answered. "I put up a pretty good fuss on both occasions, as I remember, but I never doubted your or mom's love for me at any time in my life."

"I want you to know that I could not be more proud of you. You have turned out to be exactly what your mother and I hoped you would be and more. I have no doubt that you and Jay were meant to be together. You will enable each other to be far more than what you could have been as two separate individuals."

"I'm sure that is true," Amy told her father. "And I will say this only once before I back off forever: I think the same can be said of you and Deidre. Yes, God certainly intended you and Mom have those fantastic years together. They can never be duplicated, but the Lord never intended for you to use the remainder of your days to sit around and reminisce about what used to be. You are still a relatively young man with much to offer. The Lord has someone for you, and I suppose

I could be wrong, but it appears to me there could never be a more perfect match than you and Deidre. It is very possible that just as God brought you and Mom together, He is now set to put you and Deidre together. Will you think about that, Dad?"

"Yes, honey, I have thought about that for a while now, and I appreciate your opinion and—I guess I can now also say—your permission. I don't know how a daughter of mine could have such wisdom. You are a jewel. I hope Jay knows what he has."

"Oh, he knows. I tell him all the time," his feisty daughter replied.

By the time Davis walked through the doorway to return to his apartment, there were tears of joy in the eyes of both father and daughter.

It was almost one o'clock when Davis arrived at the church decked out in tux and freshly polished shoes. He immediately went to John's study where the young preacher gave last-minute attention to the ceremony prepared for this special day. Davis had questions which were prompted by the part he would play in that ceremony. The plan was for him to walk the bride down the aisle as father of the bride and then later, as an ordained minister, to move to the platform to make a few comments before he led the bride and groom to make their vows to one another. After he made sure he had a handle on the details, he left the preacher at his desk.

Davis was almost overcome with emotion when he joined his daughter in the bride's room from which they would emerge to walk down the center aisle at the appropriate time. In his mind, no one could be more beautiful than she was at that moment. "They say all brides are beautiful," he told his daughter, "but you have broken the meter today. I presided at numerous ceremonies through the years, and I never saw a bride as beautiful as you."

"Oh, Dad, I appreciate the compliment, but you are just biased."

"I may be biased, but nevertheless it is true." He pulled her veil back to kiss her on the cheek just before they heard the music that was to signal the bride's entrance. He was very careful to get the veil back exactly as it had been. "I love you," were the words the proud father spoke to his daughter before they walked out of the room and down the aisle.

All those who filled the pews stood to honor the bride when they walked slowly down the aisle. Davis's attention was drawn to the people on the platform. Jay's best friend Grayson stood to the groom's left with three groomsmen whose names Davis could not remember, each with their hands folded together and smiles on their faces. Then he got a look at the bridesmaids. There was Amy's high school friend Emma along with Molly and Lucy, two of the young ladies with whom she had taught last year. He recognized her flower girl as little Katie, the daughter of a church friend of Amy's. Then there was Deidre who was maid of honor. Davis's heart just about stood still when their eyes met and she flashed that beautiful smile his way. Perhaps the smile was for Amy's benefit, but he interpreted it as for him and him alone.

When Davis and Amy came to a halt, the organ music ceased and the people were seated. John spoke, "Today we have come together in the presence of God to witness the joining together of this man and this woman in holy matrimony...." A couple of minutes later, John came to the question, "Who gives this woman to be married to this man?"

Davis and Amy had previously discussed how he would answer that question. The answer was, "Her mother and I." Both of them had felt that even though Julie had gone to be with the Lord, it would be proper to include her in the ceremony in this way.

Davis then turned to be seated on the second pew on the bride's side of the auditorium where he remained while John continued to lead the service. When it was time, he walked to the front where he stood beside John and faced the bride and groom to begin his comments. He fought back tears when he said, "Amy, my desire for you is that you will find the same happiness with Jay I enjoyed with your mother. Your mother, more than anyone else, taught me what it meant to truly love another. Through the years she demonstrated to me that genuine love includes not only the excitement of romance, but it means to also care as much about the welfare and happiness of your marriage partner as your own. Her love was the most important factor in my development as a person. Amy, I challenge you to devote your life to loving Jay, and thus enable him to become the best person he can be."

Then Davis looked directly into the eyes of Jay. "Jay I would remind you that nothing is easier than to repeat the words and nothing harder than to live them day by day. To say 'I love you' is one matter, to demonstrate the truth of that statement is another. The words will, undoubtedly, be greatly appreciated by Amy and therefore should be spoken often, but it will be your actions more than your words that will give her the assurance she will need all the days of her life."

Davis continued his challenge, "Love will always be an extremely important element in your marriage. It is the factor that will not only make life bearable, but also victorious for both of you. For you see, burdens are made lighter where there is love. When two people love one another they divide the burdens that come into their lives. Joys are more intense because where there is love, joys are shared. Love for one another makes you stronger. It will enable you to go where you dared not go alone."

Turning to Amy he said: "Amy, my prayer for you since you came into our home has been that you would find that life partner God has for you. As a result of my time with Jay, I am convinced he is that person. But even a match made in heaven requires work, and I encourage both of you to pay the price to make your marriage all it can be."

At this point Davis had to pause and swallow to get the lump out of his throat before he went on. "Will you now join hands and repeat your vows to one another?"

After the processional, the wedding party gathered outside before they walked around the side of the church auditorium to the fellowship hall for the reception.

It was Amy who first spotted it and called to Davis, "Look, Dad, do you know anything about that?" she said, pointing toward the sky. Overhead was a small airplane that pulled a long banner with the words, "Best Wishes Jay and Amy."

"It's Charley!" Davis said, laughing. "He told me to make sure you looked up when you left the church. I guess he is a pilot after all." At one point close to three hundred people stood in front of the church with their eyes turned toward heaven. Someone remarked, "People who pass by in their cars will probably get the idea that Jesus has returned."

In approximately two hours Jay and Amy were on their way to Atlanta to catch their flight to Orlando, and Davis had returned home to feel a little drained and let down now that all the festivities were over.

Davis was taking off his tux in favor of jeans when his doorbell rang. It was Charley.

"Sorry I missed the grand event, but the delivery of my gift required my presence. I know we were spotted because I could see people on the ground with their faces fixed on us. What did Amy and Jay think about it?"

"They were delighted, Charley. It certainly gave their wedding a unique touch. You and your airplane provided them an unusual twist to talk about in the future when they reminisce about their special day."

"Actually it was Mayor Ellison's plane. The next time you see him, you might want to thank him and his co-owners for the use of the plane without charge. To pay for the banner to be painted and rental of the plane would have been a real strain on my budget. Kenneth White, one of the three owners, even flew with me. I don't think they trusted my ability without some supervision."

"I didn't know Sam owned a plane. Does he fly it?"

"As I understand it, the three of them: the mayor, Kenneth, and Larry Payton who is the manager of one of the carpet plants in Calhoun all chipped in to buy it. It is a sweet little Cessna 172 Skyhawk, four seats. My guess is they had to chip in about seventy to eighty grand a piece. They keep it at the Calhoun airport and have a sign-up method to schedule its use. And yes, Sam does have a license. He flies some. "In fact, he was waiting for us when we landed back at the airport after the wedding, anxious to take her up."

"Evidently the old boy is better off financially than I thought. It must be his furniture business that produces the money, because I know his salary as mayor doesn't give him that kind of income. I will thank him the next time I run into him."

"Are you ready to take that plane ride with me?" Charley said, grinning at Davis. "I have a plane booked at the Calhoun airport at one o'clock tomorrow. I will have use of it for the rest of the day and that should give us time to fly over the state line to Franklin, North Carolina, where we can check out this Reed Johnson who has been so anxious to get the Ammon place."

"Is there an airport in Franklin? As I remember, it's not a very large town."

"Yes, there is. I checked it out online. It's called the Macon County Airport and seems to be a decent sort of place."

"I'm glad to hear it is a decent sort of place because I certainly wouldn't want to be with you while you landed somewhere that was a dump."

"You have nothing to worry about. I could put the kind of plane we will be in down in a cornfield," Charley said, laughing.

"I hope that won't be necessary," Davis emphatically stated. "I do plan to go to church tomorrow. Does that give us enough time to get to the airport?"

"That shouldn't be a problem if that preacher of yours doesn't preach too long. I tell you what—I will go with you to church tomorrow and we can leave from there, run through the window at one of the fast food places to get lunch, and be at the airport ready to go before one o'clock."

"That sounds great to me," Davis replied while he thought, *Anything to get Charley exposed to the Word of God, even a plane ride with an inexperienced pilot. Whatever it takes! Thank you, Lord.*

As he slept that night, Davis dreamed of him and Charley in a space craft while it rapidly fell to the earth. He awoke covered with sweat, delighted that it was only a dream. He got up for a drink of good Adairsville water before he went back to bed and forced his mind to focus on more delightful thoughts. He thought of the beautiful young woman next door. His dreams for the rest of the night were much more pleasant.

CHAPTER 16

True to his word, Charley met Davis in front of the church just before the ten thirty worship service would start. "You don't think the roof will fall, do you?" Charley facetiously asked his friend. "You know it has been a while since I've been to church."

"Yes, I know, but this roof seems to be strong enough. I think we will be okay."

"We don't have to sit near the front, do we?" Charley asked.

"No, I asked Deidre to save us a seat as near the back as possible."

"This gets better all the time," Charley remarked. "So we will sit with Deidre. I can do that."

"I will sit with Deidre. You will sit with me," Davis explained.

They immediately saw Deidre flashing that beautiful smile, seated in the next to last pew on the left hand side. Barbara sat at her side. With a defiant grin on his face, Charley swiftly moved to Deidre's side and seated himself. This left Davis no alternative but to sit at the end of the pew next to Charley. *Oh, well, at least we got him here, Lord. Please open his mind and his heart to John's message. Give John words to say that would somehow get his attention and make him aware of his need for you.*

The twenty-five minutes before the sermon was typical. Then John read his text for the day from Psalm 5:11–12, "But let all who take refuge in you be glad; let them ever sing for joy. Spread your protection over them, that those who love your name may rejoice in you. For surely, O Lord, you bless the righteous; you surround them with your favor as with a shield."

"Hurt or pain, or trouble of any kind can be a terrible ordeal, but it can also have its positive side. We don't have to just make it through tough times, we can be made through tough times. We can be made into the beautiful likeness of our Lord through those hard times, and from that perspective the pain is worth the gain. So there are times when God, for our benefit, may decide it best not to eliminate the battles that come into our lives. He will decide to use the struggle to make us better, but even then God continues to serve as our shield. He will protect us and limit the hurt to only what we can bear." Charley looked at Davis when a baby in the arms of a young mother seated just two pews in front of them started crying.

Pastor John went on, "David, who wrote Psalm five, as far as we know, was not faced with any extreme physical pain at this time. His was a wound of the heart. I suspect most of us have discovered what David obviously came to understand, such hurt can sometimes be more painful and cause more damage than even the most extreme physical wound. We find back in verse nine a pretty good indication of what seriously nagged at David, 'Not a word from their mouth can be trusted; their heart is filled with destruction. Their throat is an open grave; with their tongue they speak deceit.' Have you been there?" the pastor asked his audience. The young mother with her baby in arms and still crying got up to slide in front of the people in the pew and made her way out the back door.

"The people of whom David is speaking here in Psalm five are said to be evil, wicked, arrogant, liars, bloodthirsty and deceitful. The bottom line is that they are motivated by the sin in their hearts. We need to know that God is not indifferent toward our pain and problems. The cross of Jesus should continually remind us of that. I suppose it would be fair to say that the cross—the sacrifice of Jesus, was really about God relieving our hurt. Its purpose was victory over sin which is the source of much of our pain. When all is said and done, it is our victory over sin, which only the shed blood of Jesus can produce, that provides us serious protection."

As the young orator moved toward the conclusion of his message, he spoke with more urgency. "David understood, and I hope each of us understands that the place of comfort and relief in times of hurt is in the presence of God. Pain should not push us away from God, but rather toward him. Don't you love David's statement—'For surely, O Lord, you bless the righteous; you surround them with your favor as with a shield'? Isn't it great when we hurt, or any other time, to be surrounded with the favor of God and protected as with a shield?

"Do you need a shield? Of course you do! We all do, so you, like the rest of us, need Jesus who the Father has provided to us as that shield. Please notice this explanation in our text: the *righteous* are those who are surrounded by God's favor as with a shield. Such righteousness can only be attained through Jesus."

Davis had not turned to look at Charley when John had spoken, but he was able to see out of the corner of his eye that his young friend for whom he had been praying was engrossed in the words of the preacher.

"I had no idea that John was such a good speaker," Charley told Davis when they drove in his Jeep toward the window at McDonalds to get lunch. "I really liked the idea that God can be our shield. Look at this," Charley said, pulling his badge from his pocket. "What does this look like to you?"

"I've never noticed that," Davis admitted. "The badge is actually shaped like a shield."

"We often refer to it as our *shield*. In our business it is good to have a shield. It never occurred to me that God could be our shield. A good analogy," he declared.

Thank you, Lord, for that point of contact. The door has been cracked. Give me wisdom to walk through it in the best possible way. Help me not to hold back when there is opportunity, and not to force it when he is not ready to listen. "Yes, John is an excellent communicator and I hope you will take the opportunities you have to hear him more in the future. He can teach us a lot."

"I can do that if you will let me sit with Deidre when I am there," Charley responded with a laugh.

Charley talked nonstop as Davis drove toward the Calhoun Airport. "We still have not gotten those boys we arrested to talk about who was behind their harassment of you folks, but we did find out a little about them. Their names are Brunson and Racine. They are from over in the Canton area where they have been in and out of trouble for years. Brunson, which is the tall skinny one, has done over seven years' prison time for armed robbery. Racine has done a little jail time, but so far has escaped prison, probably only because he has not been caught. We found their camper and gear in the woods just off Pleasant Valley Road. It seems they moved around. They would find a good spot and stay there without permission until there was a need to move elsewhere. I still think when they realize it could be to their advantage they will come around."

"Have you made any progress toward getting the identity of the person they drove to the airport the night I followed them?"

"No; maybe it was Johnson. When we get to the Macon County airport, we need to find someone to question about whether Johnson has any aviation connections. He could have had a ride waiting for him at the airport that evening. He may even have a plane of his own."

Davis felt mildly anxious when he drove into the airport parking lot. He tried to hide his nervousness from Charley. His young friend would make his life miserable if he detected the least bit of reluctance about being in the air with him.

"What kind of aircraft do you have reserved?" Davis asked just to make conversation.

"Probably that one over there." Charley pointed toward a small plane to their left. "It's a Cessna 172, same as the mayor's plane that

I flew yesterday only a couple of years older. It is small with only two seats, but should be roomy enough for the two of us."

There was a ten-minute wait while Charley took care of the paperwork before they climbed into the plane. In a moment they were on the runway with the engine revved up ready for takeoff. "When will the flight attendant stand and tell us to buckle our seatbelts, point us to the emergency doors and such?" Davis's nervous humor fell rather flat with Charley who didn't bother to respond.

While they moved rapidly down the runway to begin their ascent, Davis had his hands on his knees. When he removed his hands, he noticed that he could see the handprints on his trousers left by the perspiration from his palms. The passenger was relieved that before they reached the end of the runway, the plane lifted and quickly gained altitude. Soon they were over the little town of Calhoun which is the Gordon County seat.

"I think you will enjoy the scenery," Charley told his passenger as they leveled off several hundred feet above the houses and cars below. "Most of the trip will be over the beautiful North Georgia Mountains. Just sit back and enjoy the ride."

Easy for him to say, Davis thought.

After they were in the air for a few minutes, Davis saw that Charley evidently did know, at least a little, about flying a plane, and he obviously observed all the normal precautions. Then he relaxed and enjoyed the ride. "You handle this piece of machinery like it's old hat," he told the young pilot.

"It's not hard, not a whole lot different than driving except a few more gauges to watch. The main job of a pilot is to keep his mind on what he is doing. The advantage up here is that since there is not a lot of traffic, you don't have to constantly watch the other guy."

The sky was a deep blue with only an occasional white cloud. The sun made shadows in the trees below that created a dark green effect with which Davis was fascinated. "You were right; the scenery is beautiful from up here."

When they saw a fair-sized lake, Charley pointed to the left. "That is Blue Ridge over there. We will cross the North Carolina state line in a few minutes."

It was about the time that Davis had gotten relaxed enough to thoroughly enjoy the trip that Charley announced, "We are just about there." In less than five minutes they began their descent into the Macon County Airport just outside the little town of Franklin, North Carolina. "The takeoff has never been a problem for me. Once off the ground to stay in the air is a breeze, but it is the landing with which I have a real problem," Charley jested.

Davis's palms suddenly began to sweat again, but the plane was soon safely on the ground and they taxied to the proper position. They reported in, after which Charley showed the man behind the counter his police credentials before he threw some questions at him. Charley once explained to him that even in a spot where he had no jurisdiction, to flash his identification helped people to understand he could be trusted and made it easier to get answers to his questions.

"Do you know a man who lives here in Franklin by the name of Reed Johnson?" Charley asked the stocky man behind the desk.

"Yes, actually I do. I know him because he is a regular here at the airport."

"Does he have a plane of his own?" Charley asked.

"He does, but he has been gone now for a couple of days. I believe he flew to somewhere in Georgia on Friday."

"Can you give us an address for his place? Since we are not familiar with your town, directions would also be good."

"I can do that for you. Just about anyone in town can tell you how to get to his house since it is the big place that sits on top of that mountain over there." The man pointed south. I would say it is probably the most visible residence in town." The clerk wrote the address along with brief directions which he handed to Charley.

"One more question I need to ask you: is it possible to rent a car for a couple of hours here at the airport? And if not, could you call to make those arrangements for us?"

"We can do that from right here. We don't have anything that would impress your girlfriend, but we can rent you a ride real cheap that will get you anywhere you want to go in Franklin."

"Sounds great!" Charley said. "Sign us up."

"Fill out this form and take your pick of either of those two luxurious vehicles over there. The Ford probably runs better," he said before he turned his head toward a small white Ford Focus, obviously several years old.

"If it runs best, that is the one we will take," Charley told him with a grin. "It will get us up the mountain to Johnson's place, won't it?"

"Oh, yeah, it's a great little car."

"I can see that," Charley responded sarcastically.

Charley got behind the wheel of the rental which clearly had not seen any soap or water in some time. Davis got in on the passenger side and found the lever under the seat to allow him to move the seat back, since his six-foot frame needed just a little more leg room than the last person who had ridden shotgun. Charley gave Davis the sheet of paper on which the address and directions were written. "You navigate!"

In less than fifteen minutes they were on their way up the mountain. They had spotted what they assumed to be Reed Johnson's home from a couple of different angles before their ascent toward the rather impressive residence. Charley remarked, "He must be loaded. That place is huge!"

They came to a paved driveway off to the left which, according to the directions, would take them to where Johnson lived. They were awed by what they saw when they rounded a curve. The house sitting on the side of the mountain was the biggest and one of the stateliest Davis had ever seen. "That is not a house," Charley declared. "That is a mansion!"

Charley parked the car. Both men got out and walked through a gate to start a relatively long stroll down a stone walkway to the front door. When they were about halfway between the gate and the elaborate residence, Davis thought he heard a growl, but decided he was imagining things. Then he heard it again and suddenly there was a flash of black and white as two large dogs ran from behind the house toward them barking and snarling. They were in trouble if the bite of the two animals was as bad as their bark. Davis, though he knew little about breeds of dogs, was sure these two huge animals were Dobermans.

"Oh, no!" Charley cried out and turned to run back toward the Ford Focus that had brought them to this crisis. "If there is anything I hate more than one vicious dog, it is two vicious dogs," Davis heard Charley say as he passed him. The dogs paid no attention to Davis. They sped past him and gave their full attention to Charley who was almost back to the gate when he was caught from behind by the two black canines.

CHAPTER 17

Davis briskly turned in Charley's direction, expecting to see his friend momentarily torn to pieces. One of the dogs had a small patch of material in his mouth that had been torn from the leg of Charley's trousers. Then he heard a lady's voice from behind him, "Topper, Sherman, stop that! Come here!" she shouted.

Immediately the two dogs turned to run in the direction of the attractive, well-dressed middle-aged lady who called out to them. She bent over to pet one dog and then the other before she commanded, "Go to the back! Topper, Sherman, go to the backyard." Both dogs, in obedience, turned to run in the direction from which they had first appeared.

"I'm sorry," she said, sounding sincere with her apology. "They would not have bothered you if you had not run," the lady said to Charley who was now walking back in their direction with his hand over a big hole in the back of his pants leg.

"I've had some rather bad experiences with dogs in the past, so I instinctively run in the other direction when I see one headed toward me."

"Did they hurt you?" the tall lady asked Charley.

"No, they didn't get any skin, only cloth."

"I am glad for that. They are mostly here for show, but they can be vicious with the right motivation," the lady warned.

"I can vouch for that," Charley mumbled, looking down at the hole in what used to be his best dress pants.

Davis smiled at the dark-haired lady in front of him and introduced himself. "I am Davis Morgan from Adairsville, Georgia. Turning his smile toward Charley he said, "This speedy young man here is Charley Nelson, one of our town's bravest police officers." Afterwards Davis cleared his throat.

The lady extended her hand to first Davis and then Charley before she spoke, "I am pleased to meet you. I am Margie Johnson. How can I help you?"

"We would like to see Reed Johnson," Davis spoke up, with Charley still a bit subdued probably as a result of his recent run with the dogs.

"I'm Mrs. Johnson, but I am afraid I cannot give you a lot of help. My husband and I have been separated now for almost three months. I can't even tell you his most recent address. I haven't spoken to him in over a month."

Charley was more composed now that his adventure with the dogs had passed. "Do you have any knowledge of his interest in a piece of property in Adairsville?" he asked Mrs. Johnson.

"I can guess," she responded. "I have a pretty good idea of why he would want property there. It's a long story. Why don't you two gentlemen come inside where we can sit down while we talk?" she suggested.

Davis marveled at the furniture in the huge room which they entered and was more than impressed with the beautiful oil paintings that hung on the walls. He and Charley were seated on a large red sofa.

"Can I get you a drink?" Mrs. Johnson offered. "Perhaps you would like coffee, soft drink, or maybe something stronger?"

"No, ma'am, we are on a pretty tight schedule. As much as we appreciate your hospitality, we had better get on with business. Can you tell us what you know about your husband's recent trips to Adairsville?" Davis nudged.

Mrs. Johnson was slow to speak and sat down in a chair a few feet from where Davis and Charley were seated. When she began to talk, it was in a very deliberate manner.

"I told him his fascination with that fairy tale would get him in trouble," she declared. "My husband is an engineer, a good one, who has made a lot of good investments. He is not always a very good person, but he is a good businessman. You can, no doubt, look around you and see that he is a very wealthy man. His problem is that he can never get enough. If there is a chance to obtain more, he will go after it. I guess that is called greed in some circles," she added.

Mrs. Johnson shifted in her seat before she continued, "For several months last year he worked in Brazil. There he met a man by the name of Juan Norris. I guess Mr. Norris started to trust him after he constantly worked around him for three or four months, because he told Reed a wild story that started in Adairsville way back in the early nineteenth century. According to Norris, before the removal of the Cherokee to the west, fifteen to twenty of them carried containers of gold to a cave not far from Adairsville. They knew they would not be able to take it with them when they were herded to Oklahoma or wherever, so they planned to hide it where they could ultimately return to retrieve it."

Mrs. Johnson paused for a couple of moments. When Sherman and Topper barked from the backyard, Charley quickly turned in that direction before his attention came back to Marge Johnson.

She continued her story, "Norris said the gold, which was buried in the second room or cavern of the cave, would be worth millions of dollars in today's market."

"Did the Cherokees ever return for the gold?" Charley asked.

"No, they didn't. Reed told me that only one of the Cherokees came out of the cave alive. There was a cave-in and only a teenager who had been recruited as a trusted worker escaped. All the others were buried alive."

Aha! The solution to the bones mystery, Davis shuddered. *This is awful.*

"So your husband believes the gold is still in the cave, and wants the property in Adairsville in order to claim the treasure for himself?" Charley asked.

"Yes, but there is more to the story. The young Cherokee who escaped the disaster in the cave did not go west. He hid out in the North Georgia mountains and eventually built a cabin to live as a white man. Evidently after a significant period of time passed, he was able to fool the few neighbors he had, or else they liked him enough to ignore the fact that he was an illegal Cherokee. In time he married the daughter of a poor dirt farmer who, of course, was white. He never forgot what happened in the cave and decided, probably in the late eighteen forties or early fifties, to return in an effort to get at least some of the gold. He knew he needed help, so he secured the assistance of two runaway slaves who had found refuge in the mountains." Mrs. Johnson turned her head toward the face of a grandfather clock against the wall to her left. Davis wondered if they were keeping her from some appointment.

"Am I right to assume that would have been maybe fifteen or eighteen years after the cave disaster?" Davis asked her.

"Yes, you are right. The Cherokee man would then have been perhaps thirty-five years of age, give or take a couple of years. If Mr. Norris's information was correct, the treasure hunter did not succeed in his mission. He and his two companions were discovered early in their effort. One of the runaway slaves was shot and killed. The other was captured and returned to his master. The Cherokee man himself got away, but he was wounded, which eventually led to the amputation of one of his arms. This disastrous attempt to retrieve the gold discouraged him from further tries, but he did write down directions to the cave. In order to guard the secret, he used the Cherokee alphabet to record those directions. I believe he died rather early, but left a wife and a daughter who often heard his story of buried gold and held on to the map."

Charley moved to the edge of his seat, evidently momentarily forgetting all about Sherman and Topper as Mrs. Johnson continued the story.

"Now, here is where the story gets really interesting," Margie Johnson told her visitors from Adairsville. "The daughter of the Cherokee and his wife was a lovely young woman who married a man by the name of Norris. In time they came to live in Adairsville. Her husband, Reed told me, was somewhat of a hero in the Confederate army. After the war he found life to be hard in Adairsville. That may have been partly due to his wife being half Cherokee. To make a long story short, they joined other Confederates who chose to go to Brazil rather than suffer through reconstruction. Through the whole process, the wife hung on to the map as well as the story of the gold she had often heard her father tell. The story and map were passed down by several generations of the Norris family who resided in Brazil. Eventually it ended up with Juan. He became rather obsessed with the possibility of someday traveling to Adairsville to claim the millions of dollars in gold that he felt rightly belonged to his family. Mr. Norris was a tattoo fanatic, and I understand he even went so far as to have directions to the cave tattooed on his own body so as to never lose them."

Davis and Charley silently looked at each other.

"There is still more," Mrs. Johnson informed them before her cell phone rang. She picked it up and looked at it before laying it back on the table without responding.

She continued her story. "I understand there was news reported that skeletons were found in a cave near the Adairsville community sometime before nineteen twenty. Those who knew the story of the treasure assumed that those bones were the remains of the Cherokees caught in the cave-in, but there has never been any word of the discovery of gold. Reed felt that if that much gold had been uncovered, it would surely have been reported far and wide. He surmised the treasure had to still be buried in the cave. That motivated him to make some kind of deal with Juan Norris to bring him to America. Ever since he first heard this story, Reed has been unable to think of anything else. He is convinced that finding this gold could make him one of the wealthiest men in the country."

"Perhaps you have heard that Norris did come to Adairsville where he recently died. What do you know about that?" Charley asked.

"I had not heard of his death," Mrs. Johnson replied. "I don't doubt that Reed would go to almost any extreme to gain a fortune like that, but he would draw the line short of murder."

"No one has suggested he killed anyone. Mr. Norris died of natural causes, but his body was later stolen from the funeral home and discarded along a roadside," Charley explained.

"I suppose Reed might take the body in order to secure the directions to the cave if he needed to do that, but I don't think he had any reason to. I understand he had, in his possession, a copy of the directions to the cave even before he returned from Brazil. Fact or fiction, that is all I know about the whole affair. You will have to find my husband in order to get any further information. Good luck with that," the estranged wife stated sarcastically.

"Could you perhaps give us a guess as to where we might find your husband, Mrs. Johnson?" Charley asked when they had risen from the sofa.

"I'm sorry I can't. If I had any idea I would tell you, but I simply don't have any information that would help you. I never know what he will do next. I could receive a telephone call tonight or it could be six months or next year. He is unpredictable," Mrs. Johnson declared.

Davis thanked her before they got into their rental car to travel back to the airport.

Even before they were out of the driveway, the two men eagerly discussed what they had been told. "That is a pretty wild story, but combined with what we already know, it all makes sense," Charley suggested to his companion.

"Then you think Reed Johnson is our man?" Davis asked.

"All the evidence seems to point in his direction," Charley answered. "What we heard today only reinforces what I already knew. I see no reason to come to any other conclusion. What about you? Are you convinced he is the man behind the theft of Norris's body from the funeral home and the activities of Stringbean and Sumo Wrestler?"

"I suppose I am, but there are still some unanswered questions, like what did Johnson have to gain by stealing the body if he already had a set of directions. Also his wife seemed to believe strongly that he is not capable of murder, but yet the hired help did not seem to hesitate to make an attempt on the life of another?"

"I don't know all the answers, and wives don't always know their husbands as well as they think they do, but perhaps when we get a warrant and run him down, we will learn the whole story. In the meantime, maybe we can find some connection between Brunson and Racine, and Reed Johnson. Since Johnson flies, it would seem logical that he is the person those two took to the airport the night you followed them. It all seems to come together perfectly," Charley added.

"Maybe! Johnson is undoubtedly involved, and it would seem the brains behind the whole mess, but I suppose I won't be fully convinced until we have indisputable proof."

"Regardless, we have made some real progress on this trip," Davis commented. "It has been a worthwhile afternoon."

When the two travelers arrived at the airport to return the car and start their trip back to North Georgia, the clerk informed them that someone had been there anxious to see them. "He asked about your whereabouts. When I told him you had gone to Johnson's place, he inquired about the location of your Cessna."

"Did you tell him?" Charley asked.

"Yes, I assumed he wanted to wait there for your return, and he looked harmless enough. He's probably waiting for you there."

No one was in sight when they returned to the plane. "I guess whoever it was got tired of waiting and went home," Davis suggested.

"We don't have time to wait around," Charley added. "We've got to get this baby back to the airport, or I will owe the owner more than a month's salary."

They climbed into the plane and again Davis was surprised at how smoothly Charley managed to get off the runway. "Just like a professional," Davis complimented the young pilot.

After they leveled off above the hills and trees, Davis told Charley, "You know, Mrs. Johnson's story about Cherokee gold is not so hard to believe. I have read that by the eighteen twenties some of the Cherokees had accumulated a lot of gold. You remember that this was just before the time of the Dahlonega gold rush, before most of the gold had been removed from the ground. The Indians soon realized that their personal wealth was the very factor that could destroy them, and ultimately that is what happened."

Davis reminded Charley, "It was the white man's greed for the gold that was mostly responsible for the Trail of Tears. But in the meantime, according to what I have read, they hid their gold in caves or buried it in pots made of clay or cast iron. The precise location would usually be marked by a series of signs. The signs were carved on rocks or beech trees and carefully recorded on a waybill or what we would call a map which would often be passed down from generation to generation until some family member would have the opportunity to make the long trek back to get the family fortune."

There was only the steady sound of the engine for a time as the two travelers sat silently, Charley focused on his duties as pilot and Davis almost ready to fall asleep. Then Davis noticed that the engine seemed to miss a beat or two. *Just my uneasiness about being in the air,* he decided before looking at Charley for any sign of panic. Then the engine sounded as if it was choking, starting to seriously splutter. It was then that Davis saw that look of panic on Charley's face. The pilot reached with his right hand to make an adjustment, but the engine continued to cut out and then there was nothing, no sound at all. The engine completely cut off.

CHAPTER 18

"What's going on, Charley," Davis screamed at the pilot.

"Mayday! Mayday! Mayday!" Charley cried into the radio mike. "We're going down!" The small plane rapidly lost altitude. Charley obviously was doing all he knew to do to restart the engine, but their descent continued, forcing Davis backwards in his seat. He was reaching for something, anything to hold onto. While it all took place in a matter of seconds, he felt as if he was in some kind of instant replay being shown in slow motion.

Davis glanced down to see what was below, only to observe a heavy growth of trees and bushes. It looked to him as if those trees were moving toward them and at any moment plane and trees would come together to create a collision like nothing he had ever seen before. But then there was a glimmer of hope. Just beyond a stand of tall pines on the top of that rugged mountaintop was what looked like a small clearing. *Was it really a clearing or maybe just last-second wishful hoping? Even if it was a clearing, could we make it over the pine trees and stay in the air long enough to reach that knoll? Would the small space provide length for Charley to put it down?*

Davis braced himself as he felt the bottom of the plane scrub the top of the trees and heard the scraping noise it created. He reached to tighten his seatbelt and then leaned forward in his seat. The powerless aircraft touched down and bounced several times. When Davis looked up and saw how short the emergency runway was, he had serious doubt about whether they could come to a stop before they got to the end of the clearing. Then without warning, their bumpy ride was interrupted when they hit a ditch or some kind of deep dip that caused the plane to flip forward and start to skid upside down across the knoll.

Davis had never experienced anything quite like this ride with feet in the air and head pointed down. It must have continued for at least seventy-five feet. When the craft came to a standstill, Davis was thrilled to still be alive. He then heard Charley's cry from beside him, "Get out! It could go up in flames at any minute! Get out!"

When Davis heard his friend shout, his immediate response was, *Thank you, Lord, he's alive.* He diligently started to wiggle, twist and turn in an effort to get out of his seatbelt. When that effort was finished, he fell down head first and immediately attempted unsuccessfully to open the door on the passenger side. By this time Charley had made his way out of the wrecked plane on his side. "Take hold of my hand," he called to Davis. Davis reached up toward him with his left hand, but when Charley pulled, Davis felt a sharp pain that caused him to grimace.

"Let's use the other hand," Davis said as he extended his right hand to Charley who then pulled him from the wreckage.

"Run, get as far away as possible!" Charley yelled before he broke into a sprint while he glanced back at the plane. Davis followed.

They both gasped for air and collapsed to the ground when they reached the trees fifty or sixty yards away. Charley remained seated upright while Davis lay on his back. They both looked toward the plane, expecting it to burst into flames at any moment. There was some smoke that surrounded the wreckage perhaps from the friction of the upside down skid or maybe it was steam from spills on the hot engine.

"Are you okay?" Charley asked. "There is blood on your head."

"My arm is hurting a little." Davis responded, holding his left shoulder with his right hand, "but I don't think I have any serious problems. What about you?" he asked Charley.

"I don't think there are any bones broken," he reported when he touched his arms and legs before he pulled his cell phone out of his pocket. He punched 911 and then looked at his phone in disgust, "Wouldn't you know it—no signal. Try yours," he directed Davis.

Davis reached for his own phone to find that he had the same problem. "A dead spot for cell service I suppose," he speculated.

"Well, they know we went down. I got the Mayday distress call off before we crashed. We need to stay here until rescuers come. That is the only option we have."

"It looks like we are in the middle of nowhere. I can't see any advantage to setting out on foot since we have no idea which way to go in order to find help."

"I can't believe that airplane has not burned to a crisp," Charley remarked when he noticed that the smoke was dying down. "If the insurance doesn't come through, I will pay for this little incident for the rest of my life."

"Don't worry about that now; just be thankful we both came out of it alive." Psalm five verse twelve, the passage he had heard John talk about that very morning again came into Davis's mind, *For surely, O Lord, you bless the righteous; you surround them with favor as with a shield.*

After a few minutes Charley tried his cell again, but still there was no signal. "You stay here; I think I will go see if the radio in the plane is usable," he told Davis. "If it's not, I will walk around to try to find a live spot for the cell phone."

"Be careful," Davis instructed. "That plane could suddenly burst into flames."

"No luck," Charley announced when he returned ten minutes later to the spot where Davis had remained. "The radio is shot and I tried several locations, but got no cell phone service at any of them."

"I've been asking myself some questions." Davis said. "Do you think it is possible the visitor we had at the airport, the one we failed to find, could be responsible for this?"

"It's a real possibility. You know I worked for Dean at the garage before I became a cop. I'm a fairly reliable engine mechanic. What I observed and heard seemed to me to indicate a gas line problem. I would guess the gas flow was cut off or more likely rigged to be excessive. That is a job that could have been done in a matter of moments by someone who knows motors."

"If indeed our visitor did tamper with the plane, it probably wasn't Johnson. The man at the airport desk would have recognized him and identified him as the person who asked for us."

"Maybe you are right, but men like Johnson don't usually do their own dirty work. Because he was not the sneak who tampered with our plane doesn't necessarily mean he wasn't responsible. And I am here to tell you now, whoever it was had better watch out when I get my hands on him." Charley was unable to hide his indignation over the annoying idea of an attempt on their lives.

"Do you have matches or a lighter we can use to start a fire?" Davis asked.

"I do have a lighter."

"It will be dark in an hour or so," Davis pointed out. "Do you think we ought to drag some brush and limbs from the woods to start a fire so our rescuers can find us when they do arrive?"

"That's a good idea. We ought to be able to find enough dry wood around here to do the job." It took the two men about forty-five minutes to locate the needed fuel for their fire. The strain of the task caused Davis to realize that his left arm was more affected by the crash than he had first thought. By the time the job was done, he could hardly move the arm while the rest of his body was so sore it hurt to walk or even to stand.

The two stranded men started a fire large enough that anyone in the vicinity would be able to find them. They brought out enough reserve fuel to keep it burning for two or three hours. "Not only will it draw the searchers to us, but it will also help keep the bears away," Charley suggested.

Deidre and Barbara lounged in their apartment after a light Sunday evening dinner. "It's almost dark," Deidre remarked. "Davis should have returned by now."

"It's still early, sweetheart," her roommate responded. "There is no need to worry. Those two awful guys who caused all the problems are behind bars. You'll hear that Jeep out in the driveway any minute now."

"I suppose you're right. It's just that sometimes I get these moments of anxiety that I can't shake, especially in regards to Davis. Today has been one of those days. I can't put my finger on why, but I haven't been able to get rid of this uneasy nagging that all is not right."

"It's natural to be concerned about those we love, especially when they are in the air with an inexperienced pilot," Barbara said, laughing. "I have often reminded myself of what Jesus said in the Sermon on the Mount, 'Who of you by worrying can add a single hour to his life?'"

"I guess I need to work on that," Deidre said more to herself than to Barbara. "Have you heard from Ted since he got back to Savannah?"

"No, but of course it's been less than two days since he left. He is pretty good about staying in touch. I appreciate the encouragement you gave him while he was here. It will, no doubt, be rough for him for a while, but I think he is back on track. I am sure you had a lot to do with that. I'm amazed how the Lord works. I think it was the shock of being shot that caused him to open up and talk with me. I know mothers say it about their sons all the time, but it's true in this case—he's a good boy."

"He is a good boy, and I know he will be fine. He has one of the best mothers in the world to give him the needed support."

"Thank you for those kind words. I will try to be worthy of them. As I have gotten to know Davis, I have started to understand why you feel so strongly for him," Barbara abruptly changed the subject after a pause. "He seems to be a devoutly spiritual man. Why do you suppose he left the ministry?"

"Davis is a quiet, almost introverted person. I am sure you, of all people, realize that the demands of the ministry put a lot of pressure on such a person. He constantly has to push himself to labor outside his comfort zone. It was Julie, his late wife, who took up the slack. She provided him the self-assurance that kept his confidence strong. Without her, I think he feels that as much as he loves doing the Lord's work, the ministry is outside the realm of reason for him. They were a team and with half the team gone, he feels there is no possibility of a successful ministry."

"Do you think he will ever get over that and realize the Lord can step in to fill the gap where there is a weakness? Do you think there is a chance he will someday return to the ministry?"

"My opinion is that eventually it will dawn on him that he has a strength that supersedes any personality flaws he might see in himself. But I know that even if he never returns to the ministry, he will continue to serve the Lord well. His heart is right, and I am convinced that when it is right, a person is going to serve the Lord effectively despite the occupation they happen to choose."

"I know that is true, but we need good pastors, and it pains me a lot to see one with such potential for that work walk away from it."

"I have confidence that Davis will ultimately follow where the Lord leads. That may be in the pastorate or it may be in another field, but he will continue to be faithful."

The time passed slowly for Deidre while the two ladies spent their leisure time in quietness with good books. At eleven o'clock Barbara excused herself to her bedroom. Deidre remained on the couch still concerned that Davis had not returned. *Watch over him, Lord,* she prayed. *Wherever he is and whatever threatens him, watch over him. Surround him with your favor.*

When two o'clock came and still there was no sign of Davis, Deidre knew there was a problem. Where is he? What has gone wrong? What do I need to do? *Lord,* she prayed, *give me wisdom. What can I do to help Davis?*

Deidre only dozed occasionally throughout the night. She was on her sofa where she had been the whole time when her cell phone rang at about seven o'clock. She jumped and, for a moment, hesitated to answer. She wasn't ready for bad news, but maybe it would be good news.

"Hello, Deidre." She was relieved to hear Davis's voice. "I've got a favor to ask. Would it be possible for you to drive up to Blue Ridge? Charley and I need a ride home."

"I can do that," she answered, knowing there had to be more to this story. "Where in Blue Ridge can I find you?"

"We are at the emergency department of the Fannin Regional Hospital," Davis told her.

"The hospital?" Deidre's voice was suddenly higher. "Why are you at the hospital?" she quickly inquired.

"We both are fine, able to walk around on two legs and anxious to get home. I will explain it all when you get here."

"If you both are okay, then why are you at the hospital? What is it that you are not telling me?" There was stress in her voice as she got up from the sofa and walked across the room and then back again. "This isn't the time to protect me. Tell me what's wrong!"

"I promise you, Deidre, neither one of us is seriously hurt. We had an accident and are stranded, but there is nothing to worry about," Davis assured her.

Still not fully convinced he was being totally upfront with her, Deidre told Davis, "I'll be there in a couple of hours."

"Deidre is on the way," Davis told Charley who was close to sleep perched in one of the hard blue chairs in the lounge area of the emergency section of the hospital. "Let's find the cafeteria and I'll buy you breakfast."

Davis chose eggs and ham while Charley enjoyed a stack of pancakes. "I don't think I have told you how much I appreciate the way you put that plane down on that small space on the mountain. I doubt that most seasoned pilots could have done as well," Davis remarked.

"The compliment is nice, but I really don't deserve it. We were lucky that we just happened to be near that knoll at precisely the time the engine shut down. I think the fact we hit that ditch and flipped was also luck, because I don't think I would have been able to stop it before we ran into the trees at the end of the grassy area if we had continued upright."

"I've thought about that some. I don't know that it was luck. It seems to me there was just too much that went our way to call it luck. Maybe it was a higher power that stepped in to take care of us."

"I know exactly what you are getting at, and I can't say I disagree. I have always felt pretty much in charge. I thought I could handle just about any crisis that came along, but up there in that plane above that mountain with us falling to the ground, I had absolutely no control whatsoever over my destiny. I can't get John's sermon out of my mind. He spoke of God as a *shield for the righteous*. Well, I know I am not in that group, so I guess it wasn't me who was protected, but fortunately I had one of his gang with me. While taking care of that one, I guess God spared my life too."

Davis saw a door and knew he had to walk through it. "Charley, my spiritual status is due to the blood of Jesus. It is only because I have given my life to Christ that I have any righteousness whatsoever. I am simply a forgiven sinner. You can receive that same forgiveness through Jesus. There is a great truth stated in the Bible, 'Though your sins are like scarlet, they shall be white as snow; though they are red as crimson, they shall be like wool.' (Isaiah 1:18) You can have that, Charley! You can have that forgiveness if you want it."

"I'm thinking about it, Davis. For the first time in my life I think I understand why a person needs more. Life is too hard to do it alone, and when we do seek help, why not go for the best, the One with the most to offer?"

"You've got it, Charley. You're right on target."

"Don't give up on me, Preacher. There are some rough edges I need to work through. I need some time."

"I understand that, but let me offer a word of caution: please don't feel like you have to work out all your problems before you give your life to Christ. Come to Jesus and let Him help you sort through them. What you cannot do on your own, you can do while in fellowship with Him."

"I'm almost there, but I need a little time. Let's talk more about it later," Charley told his friend.

"You've got it, buddy. There is nothing more important than to settle this matter. Just let me know when you are ready to take another step and I will be there."

The guys were back in the emergency area lounge when Deidre arrived. "What happened to you two?" she asked, near tears, looking from one to the other. She could see that Davis had his left arm in a sling and both he and Charley had a series of Band-Aids on their faces and arms.

"We were in a plane crash," Davis explained before Deidre embraced him.

"I was in the same crash—don't I get a hug?" Charley asked with a grin.

"Of course you do," she answered before she hesitantly eased away from Davis to hug Charley.

"That almost makes the whole ordeal worthwhile," Charley stated when released by the lovely young lady.

On the way back home, Deidre insisted they tell her the whole story. In tandem they told her their version of the Lost Mountain Plane Crash and the rescue that occurred just before midnight. That version was the correct one, not the one that was later greatly enhanced with bears and a long tramp over dangerous terrain. That version was the one reserved for the Little Rock breakfast group. Davis assured the concerned Deidre that the hairline fracture of his left arm was his worst injury. Charley suggested that even the sling that supported Davis's injured arm was there only to create sympathy. "You can't hurt those old geezers," he whimsically added.

CHAPTER 19

Davis moved slowly with some stiffness when Tuesday came, but he decided to ignore his aches and pains to spend some time in his bookshop. He noticed when he passed his glass showcase that the first edition copy of *To Kill a Mockingbird* was still there.

"I thought I told you to sell this book over the weekend, Janie," Davis called back to the young woman behind the counter. "Bills for the wedding will start to come in any day now. I need the cash."

"When a person has your kind of cash he doesn't have to worry about selling a few books to make ends meet," the perky clerk jested. "I hear you are rolling in it."

"I don't know who you've talked to, but I can assure you he isn't very reliable. I don't have two dimes in my pants pocket to rub together," Davis said, laughing.

"It's not what you have in your pockets, but that bundle you have in your bank account," Janie countered. "Hey, what are the Band-Aids all about?" she asked when she looked closely at Davis's arms and face and the sling supporting his left arm. "You look like you've been in a fight and the other guy got the best of you."

It surprised Davis that Janie had not yet heard about the plane crash. Usually rumors about such matters managed to make the rounds in the little town quickly. "I had a little accident," he explained in an effort to avoid details.

"It appears it was more than a *little* accident,'" she remarked. "What happened?"

"When I've got more time we can sit down with a cup of coffee and talk about it," he suggested.

"That is what I love about you," Janie sarcastically responded. "You are so talkative. It's hard to keep you quiet."

His cell phone rang while he puttered about in the shop. It was Pastor John who he heard on the other end of the line. "Davis, I need to come by to talk with you," he announced to his friend and sometimes mentor.

"Sure, I always enjoy the opportunity to spend time with you, John. Why don't you come by the shop about lunch time and I will buy you lunch down the street?"

"That sounds good to me. I'll see you in about an hour," the preacher said before he hung up.

What's on his mind? Davis wondered. *Usually when he calls I can't get off the line.*

Charley stopped by the shop before he reported for duty. When Janie saw his Band-Aids, she immediately remarked, "So you are the guy Davis has been fighting with."

"What happened?" she asked. "Both of you look like you have just gone ten rounds and came out on the short end."

"Didn't Davis tell you?" Charley asked.

"You know how he is. He didn't tell me anything."

Charley proceeded to give Janie a story about a plane crash that involved bears, wild men, Bigfoot, and a hundred-mile hike through the North Georgia wilderness.

"Is any of that true?" she asked when Davis walked through.

"A tiny bit of it," he said. "We did fall out of the sky and Bigfoot was there, but the rest of it is a figment of Charley's imagination."

Charley went with Davis to the back of his shop. "I've made all the contacts in relation to the crash cleanup," he told him. "It looks like I'll be all right with the insurance company unless their investigators decide there was some kind of negligence on the part of the pilot. I am sure that since I am a novice, they will give a lot of attention to that possibility."

"I'm sure no one will come to that conclusion. I don't know much about piloting a plane, but it seemed to me you made every effort possible to keep it in the air. I expect the investigators will find that aircraft was sabotaged. Will you be on patrol tonight?"

"Yes, I will."

"Would you like to have some company?"

"I don't know. The last time we teamed up I got dog bit and fell out of the sky into the woods. I guess it will be okay since just about every problem that could occur has already happened. Meet me at the station around five and we will give it a try."

John appeared at the shop just after the noon hour. "Would you prefer to go to the Adairsville Inn or the Italian Restaurant?" Davis asked.

"I think I would like to go to the Inn since I haven't been there in a while," John answered. They walked to the busy establishment located at the south end of the business district. Both men spoke to multiple acquaintances as they strolled in that direction.

John and Davis informed the waitress they planned to take advantage of the buffet. They filled their plates with food before they returned to their table. "So what's up? When you called me this morning, you sounded like you maybe had a serious matter on your mind. Are you ready to spill it?"

"Yes, but I need to tell you that for right now what I am about to reveal to you is confidential. I announced to our church leaders almost a month ago that I've committed myself to accept a church in Bloomington, Illinois."

"I can't say that surprises me," Davis told the young preacher. "From our perspective I sure hate to hear it, but I suppose for you it will be a greater opportunity. I knew we would not be able to keep a preacher with your talents hidden away in our little town forever. When will the announcement be made to the congregation and when will your resignation take effect?"

"The chairman of elders will make the announcement Sunday after next. Then I will preach my last sermon here one month later. The search to find a man to replace me has not yet started. It will probably require a good deal of time to find the right man. Please don't tell any of the elders I told you so, but soon after my announcement, they plan to ask you to be the interim preacher. I wanted to meet with you today to encourage you to seriously consider that request. I anticipate it will take several months to complete the search, and in the meantime the church will need someone like you in order to continue the current trend. I would feel a whole lot better about my decision if you would accept the elders' invitation." An acquaintance from church came over to greet the two men and they talked with him for a couple of minutes before he returned to his table.

Davis sat in silence for a few moments while he looked down at the table before he finally spoke in a low tone. "I'm honored, John, that the elders would consider me for that position, even temporarily. As you know, it is my home church and I love it deeply. That body of believers has had a significant influence on who I am today, but I just don't know if I can do it. I don't know if I am emotionally ready to take such a responsibility and then I have this history of Adairsville to write, which I have hardly started. My book business certainly needs a lot of my attention. I don't know if I have the time."

"I understand your reluctance, but will you think and pray about it? Your church really does need you desperately. The benefit of your experience could make a real difference."

"No promises, but I will definitely give it some thought plus make it a matter of prayer over the next couple of weeks. We will see where the Lord leads. Tell me about the church you have accepted, John," Davis requested.

"It doesn't exist yet," John told his surprised friend with a grin on his face. "A mega church in that geographic area has decided to send several hundred people to the other side of town to plant a new congregation. They will undergird the project financially. Their leaders have asked me to be the lead pastor. I will immediately assemble my own staff of four assistants. It is the kind of venture that excites me. As I see it, I could not ask for a better opportunity to make use of my gifts and fulfill my ministry goals. I hate to leave Adairsville, but I am convinced this call is from the Lord." John picked up his fork which up to now had lain on the table unused and finally started to eat.

"When the Lord calls, you have no choice but to go," Davis admitted.

The two, one a preacher on the verge of a dream venture, the other once a preacher now uncertain about his future, talked for almost another hour, mostly about life as a pastor. John reinforced his earlier request when they got up to leave, "I will pray along with you about that interim. No pressure, but I'm convinced it would be the best scenario for the church."

"I can see there's no pressure," Davis jovially responded, "but I do appreciate your opinion that my involvement would make a difference. Whether it's true or not, it encourages me."

"Incidentally," John turned toward Davis after they left the restaurant, "if I should be needed to perform the wedding ceremony for two friends I love and highly respect, I would be honored to come back and do so."

"That is good of you, but at this moment I know of no two people who have made such plans," he told the preacher who looked at him with a grin.

When Davis got back to the shop, still feeling the aftereffects of the plane crash, he sat down in the most comfortable chair he had in the store to make a series of phone calls.

First, Davis called his friend in Waleska. "Tom, this is Davis Morgan at the bookshop in Adairsville. I think I may have found that first edition of Adair's *History of the American Indians* you want. I found it online. The owner has it priced at just a little less than what I told you to expect. I would be happy to give you the online information to enable you to order it yourself. However, this seller offers a twenty per cent dealers discount which means I could order it for twenty per cent less than you, add ten per cent back in for my finder's fee, and you would still come out ahead. You tell me which way you want to go."

"By all means you order it," the knowledgeable Cherokee scholar told him. "Let me know when it comes in. Have you recovered from your plane crash yet?" he inquired of the bookseller.

"I don't have any real physical problems. Both Charley and I came out with only a few cuts and bruises."

"What about those two bad guys who were harassing your family? Have they talked yet?" Tom asked him.

"So far their lips have stayed locked tighter than the doors of Fort Knox, but I suspect the longer they stay behind bars, the more likely they will be to tell what they know."

After he talked with Tom, Davis punched the number of a customer in Cartersville who had requested an appraisal of a rare collection of signed modern first editions. The retired gentleman claimed he had hundreds of such collectibles and needed to know the value for insurance purposes. "What about Wednesday of next week? I can come by about two o'clock if that will work for you. See you then," he told the customer before he discontinued the call.

The next call made was to city hall. He hoped to catch "Sam" in his office. He needed to let the impatient city official know he had made progress on the book.

"Adairsville City Hall, can I help you?" The girl who answered the phone offered.

"This is Davis Morgan; could I speak to Mayor Ellison please?"

"I would be happy to let you talk with him if he was in, Davis, but Mayor Sam has flown his little plane to somewhere over in North Carolina. He will be back in a day or two," the secretary told him.

So the mayor is in North Carolina. I wonder why he is there. Davis caught up with his work in the shop and waited on several customers for most of the remainder of the afternoon. "I'll see you tomorrow," he told Janie when he passed through the door to start down the street to meet Charley. It was five minutes to five when he reached the lot where the police cruisers were kept, but Charley was already in the car under the wheel.

"Can't you ever get anywhere on time?" Charley grumbled.

"I'm actually five minutes early. You told me five o'clock and it is, at this moment, five minutes till. You need to learn to slow down and enjoy yourself a little. There is more to life than riding around town in a police car."

"It looks like we will have better weather than the last time we did this," Charley said, recalling the storm on the night they found the body of the tattooed man.

"Let's shoot for a smooth evening," Davis offered. "No major crisis tonight, if you please."

"That is the plan. We will ride around awhile, then later drop in at QT for donuts and coffee."

"You cops and your donuts!" Davis said, laughing.

"It is a time-honored tradition. We have to do our part to keep it intact," Charley suggested.

The two men rode around for a while before Charley pulled in beside the cemetery on the corner of Highway 41 and Poplar Spring Road where drivers were known to observe the stop signs with only rolling stops, a dangerous practice on the busy highway. "The speed limit posted on Poplar Springs is only twenty-five miles an hour which is sometimes extremely hard to observe," Charley informed his partner. "I will usually let one clocked below about thirty go on by, thirty to thirty-five we normally warn, but anyone over thirty-five gets a ticket."

"And you love that, don't you?" Davis declared.

"That all depends on who it is," Charley told him. "Last week I got to give Norman Pennington a ticket. Do you know Norman? Our feud goes all the way back to high school."

"No, I don't know Norman, but I bet the disagreement you two had was over a girl. Am I right?"

"Pretty much," Charley admitted with a smile.

Davis's cell phone rang. "I meant to turn it off," he declared. He looked at the number on the screen and realized it was his daughter. "Sorry, but I better take this. It is Amy."

"Hello," the father, anxious to hear from his daughter on her honeymoon, spoke into his phone. "How is the honeymoon?"

"Don't use that chipper tone of voice with me," the obviously irritated young lady on the other end of the line retorted. "What is this I hear about you being in a plane crash?"

"How did you hear about that?" Davis asked his daughter.

"I should have heard it from you," she almost shouted at him. "A father really should let his daughter know when he has been the victim in such an accident. Deidre told me when I talked with her a few minutes ago."

I meant to warn Deidre not to tell Amy about the crash. "It was scary, but not really that bad. Both Charley and I are okay. I've got a couple of Band-Aid-type scratches and only a hairline fracture of my left arm, nothing to worry about."

"I'm glad neither of you were seriously hurt, but I want you to promise me you will keep me informed about what goes on with you. How can I enjoy myself while away if I am worried about your safety?"

"I'm sorry, honey, I just didn't want to spoil your honeymoon. I promise you I will let you know immediately if there are any future problems."

Amy seemed to calm down some after she heard that commitment. They talked for four or five minutes longer. Davis told her he was in the car pulled over beside the road, but he did not tell her he was in a police cruiser with Charley.

After the call, when they drove away from the spot beside the cemetery where they had been stationed for the past hour, Charley noticed a gray car that weaved its way south. He got behind the vehicle to follow it down Highway 41 before he picked up the radio mike from the dash. "Katie, would you run a check on a gray, late model Buick Encore with Tennessee license plate number DP2 481?" They continued to follow the car while the driver ran off the road several times. Then came the dispatcher's voice, "Charley, that is a stolen car."

Charley turned on siren and the blue light flashed. The car up ahead accelerated and a moment later twirled left to speed north back toward Adairsville.

"We are in pursuit headed north on the Old Dixie highway just off of 41," Charley, who was now all business, spoke into the radio mike.

Here we go! So much for my hope for a quiet night with coffee and donuts, Davis lamented.

Charley, with eyes focused straight ahead, quickened the pace to reach a speed just short of ninety miles an hour on a narrow highway with lots of curves and hills. They were right on the tail of the fleeing vehicle.

CHAPTER 20

Davis grabbed hold of the first stationary object he could get his hand on, which happened to be the console between him and Charley while he made the curve in the road up ahead a matter of prayer.

Lord, I don't know what's going on, but I do know we need your help.... Davis could see the two fugitives in the front seat of the vehicle now about thirty feet ahead of them. *Whoever they are, Lord, they too need your protection. Give us the opportunity to help them.*

Suddenly the gray Encore slowed but only slightly to attempt to make a left turn onto Stoner's Chapel Road, but seriously skidded to the right. The out-of-control vehicle broke through a chain-link fence and slid sideways into a large oak. Fortunately for the passenger, it was the backseat door on the passenger side that crashed into the tree. Charley slammed on the brakes and quickly parked on the opposite side of the road from where the Buick was now out of commission.

By the time the police cruiser was brought to a complete stop, Davis had unbuckled his seatbelt to climb out of the car. Charley already had two feet on the ground. Charley barked, "You stay here!" Despite the instructions, Davis continued to run a few feet behind the younger man who was in much better shape. Before they got there, a girl dressed in black with blood on her face and arms bolted out of the car and screamed at the top of her lungs while she ran across the open field.

"I'll get her!" Davis called out to Charley, who did not know until then that Davis had followed him to the scene. "You take care of the person in the car."

"No, Davis. Stay out of this. This is police business."

"You can't get both of them. I can catch her!" Davis shouted while he continued to run toward the girl.

Davis could hear the girl he chased as she screamed and cried, "I don't want to go to jail. I want my daddy. Daddy, where are you. I need you, Daddy. Help me, I need you."

Now breathing hard, Davis grabbed the girl from the back with both hands. She turned and started to hit and scratch him while she repeated over and over, "I don't want to go to jail. I can't go to jail...."

"Calm down, young lady," Davis pleaded. "It's okay, I'm not a policeman. I am here to help you. I want to help."

The girl who Davis decided couldn't be more than sixteen or seventeen years old finally ceased to swing at him, but continued to sob the words, "I want my daddy."

After a few moments, she turned to Davis and cried, "Help me! Help me, please!" She held one arm out to examine the blood on her arms. Then she surprised him when she tightly embraced him.

"I promise you I will do all I can to help you," Davis told her. He put his arm around her shoulder to walk her back to the scene of the crash. To keep her calm, he continued to repeat softly and sincerely the words, "I will help you. I will do everything I can do for you...." Davis did not know the details of the mistakes this girl had made; no doubt there were more than a few, but at this moment he felt only compassion for her.

Charley managed to pull the teenage boy out of the car. He was obviously more critically injured than the girl, but Davis could clearly see that while he was in some pain, he was conscious. Two other policemen approached from the road where they had parked.

"The ambulance should be here in a moment. They are just kids—just two kids. I can't believe it's just two kids high on something. Sometimes my job stinks," Charley declared looking down at the ground. "Sometimes it's no fun at all."

Several minutes passed before the boy was placed on a gurney and taken to the ambulance while being guarded by two county deputies.

Before the girl was helped into the same vehicle, she raised her head to look at Davis with sad dark eyes and asked, "Will you really help me?"

"I will do whatever I can do for you, honey," he promised. "But it is important that you do everything you can to help yourself. I'll pray for you and I will see you soon."

"My name is Eva," she told him. "It's Eva Dawson. Will you call my daddy and tell him where I am?"

He pulled a pad and pen from his shirt pocket and scribbled for a moment. "I'll write your name so I will be sure not to forget it. I can assure you that these policemen also want to help you, and they will try their best to get in contact with you father before the night is over."

While they waited for the tow truck to come to remove the wreck from the scene, Charley spoke sternly to Davis. "If you want to continue to ride with me, you're going to have to learn to take orders. Didn't I tell you to wait in the car? That is proper procedure even for a police chaplain. In a dangerous situation you are to remain where it is safe."

"I know, Charley, and ordinarily I would, but this was different and I was pretty sure I was in no danger. It worked out okay, didn't it?"

"Yes, it worked out fine this time, but next time it may not turn out so well. It is always wise to follow proper procedure."

"I understand, Charley; I will try to do better in the future."

"I'm counting on that. If you don't, you will have to adjust to staying home in the evenings. Incidentally," Charley's tone became a little warmer, "I do appreciate your help with the girl. Without you I don't know that I could have dealt with her hysteria. You sure seemed to know how to calm her."

"I guess it comes from twenty-five years of counseling distressed people," Davis explained. "Sometimes you just give in to your instincts."

"I want you to know I had no choice but to chase that stolen car, especially with the way it weaved all over the road. But if I had known it was kids, I probably would have handled it a little differently. I realized it was a late model gray Buick Encore and remembered that was the description of the car seen parked behind the funeral home the night the tattooed body was stolen. Then when I was told it was a stolen car, I thought we were on to something for sure."

"You don't think those teenagers had anything to do with that, do you?" Davis asked.

"No, this car was stolen in Chattanooga just a couple of nights ago. There is no way it could be connected to the theft at the mortuary. They were just two out-of-control kids high on drugs or alcohol, foolishly in possession of a stolen car, and I almost killed them when I went after them like a wild man."

"You just did your job, Charley. You had no way to know who was behind the wheel or whether it was an adult or teen. They are banged up some now, but they are safe. I shudder to think what would have happened to them before the night was over if they had not been caught."

"I guess you are right," Charley moped. "But I don't like to see youngsters in the kind of trouble they have bought for themselves. I hope they can get a second chance and make the most of it."

"As do I. I plan to follow up on my promise to help the girl."

It was well past midnight when Davis pulled his Jeep into his drive. He took note that there was still a lamp on in Deidre and Barbara's living room. He guessed it was Deidre who was still up, perhaps with a book. He was tempted to knock on her door to talk with her about Eva Dawson, but decided against it. It could just as well be Barbara who had not yet gone to bed. He would have time to discuss the delinquent girl with her when tomorrow came.

It occurred to Davis that with all the excitement, he and Charley never did get those donuts. Since he had devoured a heavy lunch, he ate no dinner. Now he was feeling the effect of no food for eleven or twelve hours and went into the kitchen to find a snack. He noticed a sheet of paper on his kitchen counter. It was a note written in Deidre's hand.

Davis,

> *While I was putting up the groceries I got for you today, your landline rang. I took it and talked with a man who did not give his name. He asked that you call him immediately when you returned home regardless of the time. His cell number is on the bottom of this page.*

Love You,
Deidre

The note made three impressions on Davis. Deidre had picked up the things he had requested she get for him when he learned she was going to the store. That should enable him to have that snack. Secondly, and more importantly, was the way she signed the note. That would take him through the night.

The third impression was to wonder who had called and why the urgency. While glancing at the number on the paper, he punched the appropriate numbers after which he heard a gruff "Hello" on the other end of the line.

"This is Davis Morgan. I am sorry if I awakened you. I was told to return your call when I got home regardless of the time."

"That's right," the rather deep voice told him. "I needed to talk with you tonight." Davis was surprised when the man identified himself. "My name is Reed Johnson. I understand you and a policeman from Adairsville have been on my trail. Would you please tell me what that is about?"

Davis guarded his words. "We just want to ask you a few questions about a man from Brazil by the name of Juan Norris. Do you know him?"

Johnson answered with a voice that sounded a bit impatient. "Yes, I knew Mr. Norris. I met him when I was on a job in his hometown, but you probably noticed I said *knew him* rather than *know him*. He passed away; I believe the result of a heart attack, a few days ago."

"I am aware of that, but did you know his body was stolen from our funeral home?"

"No. I had not heard that, and I can assure you I had no reason to take his body. If you think I was involved with that, you are barking up the wrong tree."

"Not even for the directions in Cherokee he had tattooed on his body?" Davis asked in order to measure his reaction.

"I didn't need to get those directions off his body. He voluntarily gave them to me months ago. My copy is exactly like what is on his body."

"There is another question we hoped to ask you. Do you know two fellows by the name of Brunson and Racine from Canton, Georgia?"

"As best I can recall, I don't know either one of those gentlemen, and I am sure I have never been to Canton, Georgia. What do they have to do with Juan Norris?"

"I suspect you know it was my daughter and her husband who bought the property that you, according to their realtor, wanted for yourself. Those two men are, today, in jail for some rather vicious terrorism intended to discourage the completion of the deal."

"And you think I hired them to scare your family away? Yes, I badly wanted that property, and I would do whatever it takes to legally get it. I might even go so far as to bully someone if there was enough at stake, but I would never.... Let me repeat: I would never use violence in order to get my way in a business deal."

"Could I ask you one more question, Mr. Johnson?" Davis requested.

"No reason to stop now," Johnson replied. "Go for it!"

"We both know what those directions tattooed on Norris's chest is about. Did you talk with anyone else about what you and Norris hoped to accomplish in Adairsville?"

"That is the kind of information one keeps to himself, but I did tell my wife and I told a couple of other people whose help I needed, but I don't intend to involve them. That information is confidential."

"You have the right to withhold whatever you wish from me, but I'm not sure you can legally keep it from the police."

"Maybe not, Mr. Morgan, but the police have not yet asked me that question or any other."

"It's only a matter of time before they do, sir. They have asked you no questions yet because they have been unable to locate you; I'm sure you will hear from them soon."

"Incidentally," Johnson told Davis. "There is no reason for you to give the police or anyone else the number you called tonight. It will shortly be a discontinued line. I'll be in touch with you, Morgan."

Davis tried to call Charley, but found that his cell was off. It would have to wait till tomorrow.

After the conversation with Johnson, Davis tossed and turned for much of the night. *Was he simply an aggressive businessman who saw an opportunity to accumulate a lot of money or was he a crook who would go to just about any extreme to get what he wanted? The man admitted he knew Norris, but then he could hardly deny that, since it could easily be checked out. He vehemently denied he knew Brunson and Racine or that he had any part in their deeds, but of course he would. Who in their right mind would admit they were involved in kidnapping and attempted murder?*

It seemed so logical to Davis that the person behind all the trouble had to be Johnson, yet he wasn't sure. If the deplorable businessman wasn't behind the crimes over the past few days, then who was? Take Johnson out of the equation and there was no other suspect. Davis repeatedly pondered that question and could come up with only a couple of long shots. *I will talk with Charley about this tomorrow,* he told himself as he tried to put his mind in neutral to make it possible to get some sleep. Ten minutes later he did fall into a fretful slumber, but got very little rest before he rose early, still very tired.

CHAPTER 21

"Are we still on for Gibbs Gardens tomorrow?" Davis asked Deidre upon finding her getting out of her car as he was leaving for his shop.

"You bet we are. I have counted on it for several days. The first thought I had when I heard you were in that plane crash was, 'There goes my trip to Gibbs Gardens,'" she joked. Or at least Davis assumed it was a joke.

Davis enjoyed walking to his shop before he got his Jeep, but these days he took every opportunity to drive the vehicle he had waited so long to own. Today he drove the long way around to see if Charley's personal car was in the station lot. It was. He parked to go inside where he asked the policeman at the desk, "Is Charley here?"

The officer who Davis only knew as Pete answered, "I will get him for you." He picked up the mike for the house PA system, "Charley. You are wanted at the front desk."

After a couple of minutes, Charley appeared. "I should have guessed it was you. I was hoping for a tall blond. What can I do for you, partner?"

I need to tell you about the telephone conversation I had last night after I got home. You'll never guess who I talked to."

"Don't keep me in suspense," Charley said. "Who was it?"

"Reed Johnson."

"Really?" Charley responded, suddenly perking up. "What did he say? Was it another threat?"

"No, he called to ask why we were looking for him. He told me he had nothing to do with The theft of Norris's body and he claimed he had never heard of Brunson and Racine."

"Do you believe him?" Charley asked Davis.

"I don't know. I wouldn't expect him to admit he was guilty of stealing a corpse or that he had kidnapped Deidre or ordered a murder. I'm usually pretty good at spotting a lie, but in his case I don't know. I'm not convinced one way or the other. All the evidence seems to point toward him, but I'm just not sure."

"Until we find a better, more logical suspect, my money is on him," Charley emphatically stated.

"You're probably right, but I'm not ready to ignore the other possibilities,"

"Who are the others? I can't think of even one other person of interest," Charley shot back.

"There are a couple of people I have considered, but right now it's all speculation. It would be irresponsible to even mention their names in relation to this deal until there is more to implicate them. Let me work on it for a couple of days, and if I come up with anything concrete, I'll let you know."

"I don't like it and if I didn't feel certain that Johnson is the guilty party, I wouldn't back down. Because I think there is no chance it is someone else I will not push you, but you be careful that you don't get someone's dander up. People don't like to be accused."

"I'll not accuse anyone," Davis promised.

"Did Johnson give you any idea as to how we can reach him?" Charley asked. "We don't yet have a warrant for him, but I suspect that will come soon."

"No, he made a point to tell me we would no longer be able to reach him at the number I had. I did not catch any obvious clues to his whereabouts in the course of our conversation."

There was good news that awaited Davis when he arrived at his shop.

"A gentleman from Atlanta who called himself a serious collector called a few minutes ago to ask about your *To Kill a Mockingbird* book. He is definitely interested and plans to be here around noon," Janie announced.

"Thank you, Janie. This would be the perfect time to unload my most valuable book. I hope you were nice to him."

"You know I am nice to everyone," the young clerk retorted.

"I know that, but it doesn't hurt to remind you from time to time," Davis jested. Janie glared at him and slammed shut the drawer she had earlier opened.

The morning went slowly for Davis. For almost three hours he had only one potential customer, and she left without finding anything she had to have. Several people came in for lunch at the tearoom around 11:30 and the bookshop suddenly became a popular place to browse. To Davis's dismay only one of those browsers made a purchase, and it was a common seven-dollar mystery novel. *I hope my Atlanta man shows and likes what he finds. I definitely could use a good sale.*

The man from Atlanta did show, and he did like what he saw after he sat down and went through the rare first edition page by page. "I am sure you know this is one of only five thousand first edition copies, and many of those ended up in the hands of librarians, the worst enemies of collectible books," the collector told Davis. Evidently he was a man of means, because he did not even try to haggle with Davis over the price. He paid the extravagant posted price without question.

Davis couldn't wait to call Charley. "You owe me dinner. I just sold Harper Lee's book for twelve thousand five hundred. I won the bet," he baited the young policeman.

"Evidently they let all the inmates out of the asylum and one of them showed up at your store," he responded. "I've said it before and I will say it again: a person would have to be out of his mind to pay that kind of money for an old book. Why, I could buy a great car for that kind of money."

There were three reasons for Davis to rejoice when he left his shop later in the day. He had just received the most money he had ever gotten for any one book. He would spend all day tomorrow with the most adorable girl in town. And if that wasn't enough, Charley owed him dinner. Life was good.

When Deidre entered her apartment after her trip to the bank, Barbara was on her cell phone. So as to give her roommate privacy to finish her conversation, she quickly walked on through to her bedroom where she looked into her closet and tried to decide what to wear tomorrow. Normally she gave only brief consideration to such matters, but it was important for her to look her best for tomorrow's date with Davis. *And it will be a date,* she decided. As she thought about it, even though they had been together a lot over the past few months, there had been few of those occasions that could actually be described as dates. So this was to be a special day for her. Unable to decide on an outfit, she made her way back to the next room when she realized Barbara was now off the phone.

"How has your day been, sweetheart?" Barbara asked.

"I've had a nice day," Deidre reflected. "Mostly I've just bummed around and hung with a couple of good friends."

"You might be interested in knowing that was Ted on the phone. He gave his notice at the bank and in a couple of weeks will start a job as program director for a Savannah YMCA. He seems to be enthusiastic about the possibilities. I'm proud of him. I think it's the kind of position that will help him stay focused on the right goals. He said for me to be sure and tell you hello."

"It sounds to me like his life is finally headed in the right direction. I pray for him every day. I am sure he will come through this crisis in great shape."

Later as she prepared for bed, Deidre thought only of the day ahead.

Sleep came hard, but when it came it was good. Her dreams were of a large wedding ceremony with the bride decked out in the most elaborate white dress she had ever seen. When she had dreamed of such occasions over the past two or three months, Amy had been the bride. In this dream she saw the bride's face clearly. It was not Amy's beautiful features she saw this time. It was her own face. It was only a dream, but she awoke in the morning wishing she could go back to sleep and pick up where her dream left off.

The man lay in his bed alone, unable to sleep. *It looks like it is slipping away. I want that gold and I will get it! I've never been a man who gave up easy, and there is too much at stake to do that now. There has got to be a way. Morgan thinks he is smart, but he doesn't know who he is dealing with and I have right on my side.*

He thought about the two men in jail, Brunson and Racine. *I need to do something to keep them from selling me out. They will sing like birds if they think they can save their own hides. I should have known better than to hire them, but it's not like I had a lot of choices. Tomorrow is another day. I'll find a way.*

Still unable to sleep, he turned on the bedside lamp and took a book from the table. *This is one pleasure no one can take away from me.*

CHAPTER 22

Mayor Ellison appeared in Davis's shop on Thursday morning. "I hear you recently tried to call me." Sam seemed always to speak about two notches above normal volume. *Maybe that is the politician in him,* Davis decided.

"It wasn't important Mr. Mayor. I just wanted you to know I am seriously at work on the book."

"I'm glad to hear it. When do you think it will be ready?" the mayor asked.

"Well, Sam, I don't know if you have ever written for publication, but it doesn't come that easy. It takes time. I'm on it, but you can expect it to be a while yet."

"Just do your best, and let me know if you need any information from me. I will be glad to provide what I know."

"Thanks, Mr. Mayor, I'll remember that. I understand you were over in North Carolina recently. Where exactly did you go? I spent some time there a few days ago myself."

"Oh, I was with some family I have in the northwestern part of the state." The mayor looked away as if embarrassed. "I've got a lot of work to do. You have a good day," he said, already on his way out the front door.

"Since you are a preacher of sorts, I guess you don't keep up with the local gossip," Janie told Davis a few minutes after Sam left. "I heard you ask the mayor about his visit to North Carolina. The word on the street is that Sam's family over there all live in Cherokee at the Casino, if you know what I mean."

"I think I know what you mean, Janie, but like you say, I don't keep up with the gossip."

"Okay, if that is the way you feel, I will let you continue in your ignorance." The young clerk stomped back to her post.

Davis relaxed in a chair in his shop while he enjoyed the soft music that came from the speakers. In the quietness of the moment, he began to think, *There may be a way to determine if either one of those people are guilty.* He pondered his idea for a few minutes and was able to work out the details of a plan in his mind. *It is a long shot, but it just might work,* he decided.

He took the cell phone from his pocket and called Charley. "Charley, I know a way we might be able to flush out the person behind our troubles. I have legitimate reasons to call both of the people I suspect. What if I casually mentioned in those calls that I thought I had discovered a way to get into the cave and I planned to check it out at a particular time? Don't you think if the guilty party happens to be one of them that he or she will show up at the appropriate time to see what I discovered?"

"I think that could very well happen," Charley agreed. "Whoever is behind this will not likely let any opportunity to get his hands on that gold go by. But Davis, you would be putting yourself in serious danger. I don't think this is a good idea. I probably would have to look for a new job if this backfired and the chief found out about it. And what about Amy? She will have my hide if she learns I allowed you to place yourself in such danger. I'm already in deep trouble with her over that plane crash."

"Here's the plan I've come up with," Davis continued, ignoring Charley's caution. "I'm tied up for the remainder of the day, but I will call both of them after I get off the line with you. In the course of the conversations, I will mention that I have located what seems to be a small entrance to the cave and plan to explore it tomorrow morning at ten thirty. You could be parked nearby where you would not be seen by either of the people of interest that might possibly show up. Incidentally, one would come from the east and the other from the west. I thought you might need to know that to make sure you are well hidden. I can keep my cell phone in my hand with you on the line. That way I can let you know immediately if there is trouble. What could go wrong?" Davis asked.

"A lot could go wrong. You could be killed. Whoever is behind this has already demonstrated he is capable of murder."

"You will be nearby to swoop in and rescue me if anyone gets rough. I trust you. You have never let me down."

"What about the time between your emergency signal and the time I get there? That is plenty of time for some gold hungry bad guy to commit murder."

"I can keep whoever shows up occupied until you get there. You just find a good place to hide before ten thirty and make sure you get to me as quickly as possible if I need you."

"But, Davis you...." This time Davis discontinued the call and refused to answer when his phone immediately rang and Charley's number was on the screen.

Davis immediately made the telephone calls and casually dropped in the information about going to the newly found cave entrance at ten thirty the next morning. Now he would just have to wait to see which one, if either, showed up. Davis would stop by for Deidre in an hour or so for their afternoon together. He decided it best not to tell her about tomorrow's plan. The last thing he wanted to do was spoil their time together. This afternoon he would keep his mind off bad men and their crimes. Perhaps tomorrow would be the day when it all could be put to rest, and he could again feel good about the safety of Deidre and his daughter. Today, however, was for him, and Deidre and he would make the most of it.

Neither Deidre nor Davis had been to Gibbs Gardens which is a relatively new North Georgia attraction near Ball Ground in Cherokee County. The one-hour drive east was made more pleasant by the exceptional weather on this mid-summer day. It was still hot, but there was a pleasant breeze and a few clouds that occasionally blocked the rays of the sun.

"Tell me what you know about the gardens." Deidre requested.

"Not a lot, just what I read online," Davis told her. "It is spread over two hundred twenty acres that includes sixteen different types of gardens. Of course, the major attractions are the flowers and bushes with a number of species in bloom at any given time throughout the growing season. The article mentioned that musical programs are sometimes offered. Today classical musicians will stroll through the park to entertain the patrons."

"Sounds delightful," Deidre enthusiastically responded. "And very romantic," she added with a smile, as she moved a little closer to Davis. They sometimes chatted but often sat in a comfortable silence until they reached their destination and were directed to a parking spot by an attendant. Obviously it was a big day on the schedule, because the lot was almost full.

The couple listened to the brief lecture about what to expect and then opted to walk the tour rather than take the tram. "I need the exercise," Deidre explained. "And besides we are less likely to miss any of the important sights if we are on foot."

Davis pointed to the water lilies that bloomed in one of the ponds. Deidre loved the hydrangeas that seemed to be everywhere. "I don't know much about plants and flowers, but what a beautiful place this is." Davis observed what was around him in awe.

"Look at the roses. I thought they would be completely gone by now. And the size of some of those ferns is unreal," Deidre gleefully pointed out. "Thank you for bringing me," she said when she took his hand and kissed him on the cheek. "This is special." They strolled along the trails hand in hand; occasionally one of them pointed out some amazing plant to the other. After a time they were seated together on one of the benches that occasionally appeared along the way.

"I guess Amy and Jay will get home sometime Sunday," Deidre remarked while she looked out across the pond.

"That is the plan," Davis answered. "I sure wish this thing about their purchase of the Ammon place could be put to rest by the time they get home. I don't think I can get over being concerned about their safety until whoever is behind all the trouble is apprehended. I would encourage them to stay away a little longer if I didn't miss them so badly."

"Charley won't let up until they get the person behind it, and I don't think he will let any of the other guys in the department forget about it either," Deidre said.

"You're right. Maybe it's the father in me. I once knew a lady who I was convinced could not be happy unless she found something to worry about. Sometimes I think I am just as bad as her. I have often counseled people to put their concerns in the Lord's hands and trust Him. I need to learn to practice what I preach. But it is awfully hard to let go when it is your own flesh and blood who is in danger."

When they got up to continue along the trail, they went up the hill in the direction of the manor house. They found an impressive stone house predictably landscaped with beautiful trees and bushes. Since the climb up the hill was a bit strenuous, the couple sat again, this time under a sheltered area that featured a small pool. Deidre snuggled up to Davis and placed her head on his shoulder. He put his arm around her. The sound of beautiful music came from the back of the house. The music moved closer. It was one of the musicians who had been assigned to stroll through the park. This minstrel's instrument was a violin and he played a piece Davis had heard many times but could not remember the title. "This place is magical," Deidre declared. "I expect to see a unicorn pass by at any time."

Davis turned his face toward her and their lips met for a long lingering kiss. Suddenly it was no longer classical music they heard, but rather the beautiful romantic Cole Porter song, *True Love*. Davis could almost hear

Bing Crosby singing to the adorable Grace Kelly. There was a smile on the face of the violinist when Davis looked his way. "He's right you know, it is true love," he again kissed the beautiful lady at his side.

Darkness had already set in when they finally left the lot for the trip home. They were tired from all the walking, but were left with memories that would, no doubt, be stored in their hearts for a long time. Deidre dreamingly declared, "The day could not have been more perfect," and then she leaned back to take advantage of the headrest. Even the drive back to Adairsville provided the couple with special moments to treasure.

After he debated with himself much of the day over what to do, Charley finally called the chief to explain Davis's plan for tomorrow.

"What should I do?" Charley asked his boss. Should I let him put his life in jeopardy by allowing him to go through with his scheme, or should I lock him up if that is what it takes to keep him away from that property at ten thirty in the morning?"

Charley assumed the moment of silence that followed was Chief Hanson pondering his question. "Let him go ahead with it, and I will accompany you to help with your part of the plan," he finally responded. "I don't think we have anything to worry about. There is no doubt in my mind that the man we are after is Reed Johnson, and since he is in no way involved in Morgan's plan tomorrow, what could happen?"

"I see your point, sir, and I pretty much agree with you, but what if Davis is right? What if it turns out that one of his people of interest is actually our man? He could find himself in deep trouble."

"We won't even consider that possibility." Chief Hanson replied. "Who are these two suspects anyway? Do you know who he plans to con? I can think of no person beyond Johnson who could possibly be our man."

"He hasn't told me who they are," Charley told him. "I am as much in the dark as you."

"Okay, I am sure it is a waste of time, but we will drive out to Folsom at nine thirty and keep the patrol car hidden while we wait for his call," the chief told his young officer. "That way, even though we have no jurisdiction out there, we keep everyone happy and safe. I do appreciate that you brought this to my attention. It was the right thing to do."

After he got off the phone with the chief, Charley felt a little guilty, like maybe he had betrayed his friend's confidence, yet he agreed with Chief Hanson. *It was the right thing to do.* When Davis recruited him to be a part of his plan, it became police business, and since that was the case, the chief needed to be informed. Charley didn't want to jeopardize the career that brought him so much satisfaction. He intended to spend the rest of his life in law enforcement.

Charley wished he were on duty tonight. The worst loneliness of his life occurred at those times when he was home alone. Tonight would be one of those dreaded evenings. There were places he could go to party. In the past he would have chosen that option, but he didn't seem to find as much enjoyment in such activity as he once had. He wondered if Davis's prayers had anything to do with that. He would never admit it to his friend, but it was a fact that his friendship with Davis had brought some real changes to his life, *changes that were definitely needed,* he told himself. Charley had known a lot of Christians through the years, but Davis seemed different from most of them. He was real. *Davis Morgan isn't a phony, and besides that, he doesn't push. He let a man make up his own mind.*

There was a girl about whom Charley felt deeply. A pretty face? Yes, as beautiful as any he had ever known, but it was more than that. He knew if the opportunity ever came his way, he would not let her get away. She was the kind of woman to whom he knew he could commit forever. With such a girl, he would never experience loneliness again. It was this dream that occupied his mind as he listened to the silence around him. He understood that there was absolutely no way that girl could ever be his, but that did not keep him from dreaming. He wished there was some action he could take to eliminate that awful loneliness. The TV didn't get it done, neither did the music he played.

Charley spent the night in his big easy chair, thus he awakened a little stiff when dawn came. He went to his small kitchen for a cup of coffee, but decided since it was still early and he didn't need to be to the station until eight, he would stop by the Little Rock for breakfast. Perhaps Dean would be there with the other guys. He showered and put on his uniform before he left his apartment. It was a day like all the others. Or was it?

CHAPTER 23

It was not yet daylight when Davis awakened. He lay in the darkness for a while and thought about what was ahead for him that day. Had he made the right decision? Even if he were right about one of the men he had set up being the culprit, would his plan work? He hoped it would turn out that both people were innocent, but he doubted that would be the case. He had not talked with Charley since he told him his intentions, but he was confident the young policeman would be there if he needed him. Charley was a friend indeed, and Davis recalled what the Bible said, *A man of many companions may come to ruin, but there is a friend who sticks closer than a brother.* (Proverbs 18:24) Charley was that kind of friend. He didn't have to worry about whether or not Charley would show. When the time came he would be there.

When Davis selected his clothes for the day, he remembered how thankful he was that he had worn a long-sleeved shirt when he had once been chased through the woods where there were briers to grab at him. Today he chose a long-sleeved blue shirt to wear with his jeans though the temperature would surely rise to the mid-nineties on this midsummer day. Sneakers were the proper footwear because of the possibility that running could become part of the day's activity.

A cup of coffee and a cinnamon roll that remained from the groceries Deidre had brought him made up Davis's breakfast. He waited for the time to pass before he would be due to arrive at Folsom. Davis took some time to talk with the Lord and asked for His help. *Lord, you know I can be impatient and get ahead of You at times. I hope that is not the case today, but Father I know even if it is, You are a Father who protects His children even in the midst of their mistakes. I can't carry out these plans today alone, but I know I don't have to....*

While in seminary, a professor who led one of Davis's classes required his students to commit Psalm 46:1–7 to memory. At the time it was just an assignment he had to complete, but as the years went by, he was glad the professor made it a mandatory part of his class work. He often found that passage, first planted in his mind and then in his heart, to be useful in many different kinds of situations. Today was one of those days when he needed to repeat those words in his mind and experience the strength they offered. *God is our refuge and strength, an ever-present help in trouble. Therefore, we will not fear, though the earth give way and the mountains fall into the heart of the sea, though its waters roar and foam and the mountains quake with surging. There is a river whose streams make glad the city of God, the holy place where the Most High dwells. God is within her, she will not fall; God will help her at break of day. Nations are in uproar, kingdoms fall; he lifts his voice, the earth melts. The Lord Almighty is with us; the God of Jacob is our fortress.*

When nine thirty came, Davis knew it was time. He remembered that other time when he had battled a villain, one he knew as the *Rat-faced Man,* he had used a weapon. He owned no gun and knew it would be useless in his hand anyway. He would never be able to pull the trigger against another human. He doubted that he could intentionally kill another even in an effort to save his own life. But this weapon had come in handy on that other occasion and it might prove to be helpful today. He went to the closet to pull out his trusty Louisville slugger, a thirty-three-ounce wooden baseball bat he had kept since he played American Legion baseball as a youth.

Deidre heard Davis walk across the front porch and parted the curtains to look out the window. When she saw that he walked down the steps with that baseball bat in his right hand, her heart skipped a beat. *Oh, no! What is he up to with that bat?* She watched him take the bat into the Jeep with him before he backed out of the driveway to head north. She turned away from the widow and met Barbara who was about to enter the living room from her bedroom where she had just made her bed.

"What's the matter, honey?" she asked. "You look like you've just seen a ghost."

"In a manner of speaking I guess I have," she told her roommate. "Please pray for Davis. Pray for his safety."

"What's up? Is he in some kind of trouble?" she inquired.

"I don't know exactly, but he just left the house with that baseball bat, and I know that can't be good."

"Well, maybe he plans to play some baseball," Barbara said, looking puzzled.

"No, it is not baseball he has on his mind. He has planned something, but it is not a baseball game. I just wish he would talk with me, tell me what he's up to. I could cope better if I knew what was on his mind. At least I would know how to pray for him."

"I don't know what this is all about, but it's my guess Davis hasn't talked with you because he wants to spare you the worry," Barbara suggested.

"You're right. I know that, but I want him to understand that I am not some fragile flower who will fall to pieces at the gentlest touch. I am a woman who has not had it easy for most of my twenty-nine years, and I would like to think I have developed some toughness, mentally and otherwise. The Lord and I can handle whatever comes along, and I want Davis to know that."

"I think he does know that and I believe he admires that characteristic in you, but Davis is a bit old school, the Southern gentleman. He has the idea that the man should spare the woman he loves any pain that can be kept out of her life, and I hope you understand what a blessing that can be for you in your life together."

"I guess you're right, but I want us to face these problems together. I don't want protection. I want to be part of the solution," she declared. Deidre didn't know which was her stronger emotion in regards to Davis at that moment—anger or concern. Whichever it was, she knew it was exceeded by her love for him. Throughout much of the morning she prayed for his safety.

Nothing seemed out of the ordinary when Davis drove onto the property his daughter and son-in-law had recently purchased. Davis stopped in the drive and took out his cell phone to call Charley.

"Hello, Charley, I hope you are in, or somewhere near Folsom."

"We've got your back, Davis," Charley assured him. "We are less than five minutes away."

"Perfect," Davis expressed his approval. "I will keep my phone hidden in my left hand so you can hear what is said. If anything significant happens, I will yell for your help." Davis noticed that Charley used the pronoun *we* which caused him to wonder who was with his him, but he continued on his way without asking.

He steered his Jeep straight to the area well past the house near the southern property line where he had earlier decided the cave must be located. Still he saw no signs of anyone who might be there to harm him. If someone was around, they had hidden themselves well. Davis turned the ignition to kill the engine. He looked in all directions after he had walked a few steps from his vehicle.

Just in case someone was there, he needed to play his part well. He walked back to the Jeep for the fifty feet of rope he had placed in the vehicle earlier. A man who planned to crawl around in a cave needed rope, and even though he had no such plans, he needed to make anyone who might be watching him believe he did.

Davis continued to play his part. He walked around to look at the large rocks. He even got on his knees to make anyone hidden in the bushes think he was scoping things out. Finally, he walked over to a hole between several rocks, big enough for a man to get into even though the hole could not be more than five feet deep. He wanted the culprit, if he was watching, to think this was the alternate entrance he had discovered.

To add a touch of realism, he came back up to the surface and tied his rope around one of the rocks before he dropped the other end into the hole. It was then that he realized he was not alone. An object whizzed past his head. It came so close that he felt the breeze from its high speed on his neck. He turned. The object that had hit a rock just past him was now on the ground. He suddenly realized what it was: it was an arrow, and it was the real deal with a sharp point, not a child's toy. Davis immediately fell to his knees in the hole. He shouted into his phone, "Charley, I need you! Someone just shot an arrow at me. I need you to get here now!"

When Davis raised his head to take a look, another arrow zoomed over his head. *This could get serious,* he decided. *Whoever is out there probably knows they can come down on me anytime they choose because I have no weapon.* He remembered his baseball bat, still in the Jeep, but it didn't matter, he decided. It would be of no value against arrows. *I've got to get out of here, but if I go far Charley will not be able to find me.* He decided the best move he could make was to try to circle the immediate area with as much speed as he could muster. He lifted himself out of the hole and ran full speed toward the trees that were near him. He zigzagged as he went in an effort to dodge the arrows that occasionally flew past him.

Davis managed to get to the growth of pine trees where he turned and ran to the right. After he ran a couple hundred yards he was completely out of breath, and since he had detected no arrows in the last couple of minutes, he stopped to rest and to look behind him for his pursuer. He saw no one. In a few moments he started to jog again in the direction he had originally headed. He then came to a frightful realization. He no longer had his cell phone in his hand. Somewhere along the way, while he fled from this villain, he had lost his cell phone. That left him with no way to communicate with Charley.

He only had a second to consider the possible repercussions of his situation, because, at that moment, he heard a bloodcurdling scream that brought instant terror to his heart. Then someone, presumably the person behind the scream, quick as a cat came out of the bushes to his left to pounce on him. Both men fell to the ground and Davis quickly rolled on his back in an effort to protect himself. He saw that his attacker wore no shirt, buckskin pants, and moccasins. Worst of all, however, was the tomahawk he held in his right hand which rapidly moved down toward Davis's skull. Davis was able to get his hand around the wrist of the character who attempted to pound his brains out with the stone-headed weapon. It took all of his strength to stop the hand with the tomahawk just a foot or two away from his face.

His next move surprised even him. Even with his injured left arm, he was able to conjure up enough strength to shove the attacker down the red clay bank of the hill where they struggled. Free for a moment, Davis got up and ran. He had a good start on his pursuer by the time the strange ruffian made his way back up the hill. He found speed he didn't know he possessed. It was run fast or die. As much as he looked forward to Heaven, he still had some plans for this life.

When he no longer heard his pursuer behind him, Davis stopped for a breather. He fell to one knee, and then he saw, not twenty feet away from him, the worst scene he could imagine for one in his situation: the Indian-like figure stood with bow drawn and arrow pointed straight at him. He decided at that moment that it was over. There was no way out. Still on one knee, he simply closed his eyes to wait for the arrow. Maybe the sharp instrument would enter a nonvital part of his body, or else find one of his vital organs to spare him a lot of suffering.

CHAPTER 24

Davis anticipated that the arrow would go through his body at any moment, but then he heard the sweetest voice he had ever heard. "Put that bow down or I will put a bullet right between your eyes—and don't doubt for a moment that I can do it." It was Charley, and not a moment too soon.

The man in front of Davis didn't move a muscle with bow in hand and arrow continuing to point directly at him. The Indian-like figure then glanced toward Charley, causing Davis to wonder if he was about to test the policeman's marksmanship. Then reluctantly he leaned over to put his bow on the ground.

Davis stood and looked toward his friend with a broad smile on his face. "Where have you been?"

"I got here in time, didn't I?" Charley calmly stated.

"About two seconds longer and it would have been lights out for me," Davis argued, "but I am so glad to see you—I could hug your neck."

"You do and I will turn this gun on you," Charley responded as he glanced toward the gun in his right hand now pointed toward Tom Landerhorn.

Charley pulled Tom's hands behind his back to place his cuffs on the Cherokee scholar's wrists.

While they walked back to their vehicles where Chief Hanson waited for them, Davis could not resist the urge to ask their captive, "Tom, why did you do it? You pretty much had it all. Why stir up all this trouble and even attempt to take the lives of innocent people like myself and my son-in-law?"

"Innocent? You people aren't innocent. You have stolen from us for centuries. We had every right to that gold. It's rightfully ours," the obviously off balanced prisoner responded with bitterness in his voice.

"If there is, in fact, any gold there, then you may be right, but you didn't have to attempt murder to stake your claim."

"This would have been no different than any of the other times. You overran our land, stole our homes, and murdered our people. From the time you came here you have systematically tried to destroy us. Why should I show any mercy?"

Davis couldn't argue with his logic, but he also knew there is no situation that requires murder in order to right a wrong. It was obvious that his professor friend definitely needed psychiatric help.

Back at police headquarters in Adairsville, they waited for Bartow County sheriff's deputies to arrive to transport the prisoner to county lockup. "What made you suspect Landerhorn?" Charley asked Davis.

"There were a number of clues that pointed to him. First, Johnson told me he and Norris talked with a couple of people they thought could possibly help them in their search for the gold. I asked myself, 'Who would likely be of more use than someone who knew just about all there is to know about the Cherokee in North Georgia?' Very likely it was that visit or visits that got Tom interested and first made him aware of the written directions to the cave."

"And when Norris died, Landerhorn, who knew where the directions could be found, stole the body to get those directions," Charley speculated.

"Yes," Davis responded. "And as I am sure you remember, the body was dumped not far from Oothcalooga Church on Woody Road beside Oothcalooga Creek. That is the area near where the original Cherokee village was located. Remember? The original village was north of the present site. I knew Tom, the accomplished Cherokee scholar and collector, would be familiar with that part of our community. He probably had done some excavation near there in the past. Do you remember the type of car that was spotted in the back lot of the funeral home on the night the body was stolen?"

"How could I forget after I chased those teenagers in that gray, late model Buick Encore because I thought it was that vehicle?" Charley asked.

"Did you notice what was in Tom's drive when we visited his house in Waleska?" Davis asked in an effort to stimulate the memory of his friend.

"No, I can't say I noticed."

"I didn't put it together at the time, but I did catch that it was a gray Encore, and that registered with me later when clues started falling together."

"Okay, you have already demonstrated that you are more observant than I am. What else caused you to suspect him?"

"Perhaps the most obvious clue was when I called to inform him I had found the book he wanted. He asked about whether we were recovered from the plane crash as well as about the status of Brunson and Racine. I had to wonder how he knew about such details if he was not involved."

"I don't feel so bad that I missed that one since I did not hear those slips on the phone," Charley related.

"There is more," Davis went on. "The fact that Brunson and Racine were from Canton which, of course, is just down the road from Tom's home in Waleska, caught my attention. Then when I learned that Tom was also a pilot, that he sometimes rented the very plane in which we went down, I decided that we might have gone past coincidence. I guessed it was Tom I saw Brunson and Racine deliver to the Calhoun Airport the night Deidre and I were at the grocery store."

202 | DANNY PELFREY

"I have to admit that it's not hard to see it now in hindsight, but Davis, I've got to tell you that to catch all of that on the run was pretty impressive. Sherlock Holmes could not have done better," Charley suggested. "Why do you think Landerhorn sabotaged our plane?"

"I suspect he was afraid we had gotten too close to him. He probably didn't know whether or not we had talked with Johnson. He knew that if our person of interest revealed to us that the two of them had conversed about the cave and the gold, he could be in deep trouble. Incidentally, a little investigation revealed that Tom has a cabin near Highlands, which is just a few miles from Franklin. When he learned, by whatever means, that we had planned to pay our prime suspect a visit, he probably drove to his cabin for the weekend to have easy access to us, or more correctly to our plane. The description given by the airport clerk of the suspicious man who asked about us, or as it turned out, for our plane, fit Tom as well as Johnson."

"Do you think Landerhorn planned to kill Reed Johnson to keep him away from the gold?" Charley asked.

"I don't know, but it would seem that if he were able to eliminate Jay and Amy's claim to the property, he would still have to deal with Johnson. That would be hard to do without killing him unless they made some kind of deal"

"Just one more question," Charley said. "Who was your other person of interest?"

"We don't need to talk about that now. As it turns out he was not involved with this mess, and it would be inappropriate to point a finger at him now."

"Come on, Davis, this is ole Charley you are talking to. We don't have secrets from one another."

"Of course we do. I have lots of secrets I would never reveal to you, and I am sure the same is true of you. There are facts from your life you will never tell me."

"I promise I will tell no one else. Only you and I will ever know who your second suspect was."

"I don't know; maybe I shouldn't...."

"Of course you should. Now tell me, who else did you suspect?"

"Okay, if you promise not to tell him or anyone else I'll tell you. It's just between you and me. Okay? It was Mayor Ellison."

"Mayor Ellison?" Charley cried out in surprise with a voice loud enough for people in all the other rooms to hear. "How could you suspect Sam?" Then in a low voice Charley suggested, "He's not smart enough to come up with a plan like this."

"Of course he is. He is the mayor, isn't he? He was smart enough to get elected, and he is smart enough to run our town in a reasonably acceptable fashion."

"I guess so, but I wouldn't have thought of him in regards to this mess in a million years. What made you think he was involved?"

I don't know that I really thought he was, but there were a couple of facts that made me suspicious. I found out he flies, which made him the possible passenger in that ride to the airport. Also he was actually in North Carolina when our plane crash occurred. He seems to spend a lot of money, and you will find yourself in deep trouble with me if I learn you told this to anyone else, but I understand Sam likes to gamble, which could create a real need for a few pots of gold."

"Maybe it wasn't so far-fetched to consider him a suspect," Charley said, laughing. "Wouldn't it have been fun to arrest the mayor?"

"I'm glad we didn't have to do that," Davis responded.

Later in the day Davis sat on his front porch with Deidre when he recalled that in his mad scramble to get away from Tom, he had lost his phone. "No wonder it hasn't rung in the last three or four hours," he speculated. "It's probably still out there. Would you like to ride with me out to Folsom to see if we can find it?" he asked.

"A ride in the country might be nice," she told him. Upon arrival at the site, they immediately started trying to retrace his escape route, but it wasn't easy to recall exactly where all his zigzags had taken him. As they walked with their heads turned to the ground in an effort to find the lost phone, Davis, at various points, gave Deidre a firsthand account of the chase.

"You could have been killed!" Deidre suddenly said with emotion in her voice. She almost ran the four or five steps to Davis to hug him tightly. "Do you know how close you came to being murdered out here?" She then released Davis with an angry little shove. "Don't you ever intentionally put yourself in that kind of situation again! You could have been killed," she repeated with tears in her eyes. "You could have been killed, and I would have been left all alone."

Davis embraced her, surprised at her outburst that seemed so out of character for the usual calm and kept-together woman who was the center of so many of his thoughts these days. *She loves me,* he concluded. *She really loves me. That is why she is so upset. She loves me.*

"Deidre, honey, I promise you I will never again intentionally do anything that I believe could cause you hurt. I love you, and my great desire is to make you happy."

"In that case just hold me," she responded with a hint of relief in her voice. "Just hold me for a couple of minutes."

Davis was happy to comply.

They finally located the phone in a patch of honeysuckle not thirty feet from where Davis had climbed out of the hole to start his getaway. On their way back home, the phone that they had earlier picked up off the ground rang. "Davis, this is your favorite policeman. I thought you would be interested in what we learned this afternoon," Charley told him. "Tom Landerhorn is indeed a Native American scholar with impressive credentials, but here is the bombshell: best we can tell he has no significant Cherokee blood at all. In fact, he has no Native American blood that we can trace."

"I don't believe it!" Davis responded when he digested that piece of surprising information. "It would seem Dr. Landerhorn became so engrossed in his study of the past that he placed himself right in the middle of the history he learned. He may very well have convinced himself that he is a full-blooded Cherokee. It would appear to me that he lost all perspective somewhere along the way."

"It would appear to me that he is off his rocker," Charley suggested. "You won't believe this, but after all that has happened he requested I pass on to you that he still wants to buy the Adair book."

"I'm glad," Davis said, laughing. "I've got a lot of money invested in that deal." Then without another word from Charley, there was no one on the other end of the line. "I wonder why he does that," Davis turned his head toward Deidre.

"Does what?" she asked.

"Oh, it's not important" Davis told her. "It's just that, in some ways, Charley is rather peculiar."

"I won't argue that point," Deidre said, laughing. "But I think he is probably as good a friend as a person could have."

"He is that indeed," Davis agreed. "He is that. A man could not expect to have better."

The couple went to dinner at the Adairsville Inn which was crowded with patrons, but they mostly saw only one another. The next hour brought times of quietness and moments of much chatter, but for the two of them it was all just about perfect.

"This is to be kept confidential for a few days," Davis informed Deidre, "but John will soon resign his ministry here, and I understand the church leaders intend to ask me to fill the pulpit while they look for a preacher. That search could go on for months, and since we will be married soon, I need to include you in that decision."

Davis's statement was so matter-of-fact that Deidre almost missed it. "Wait a minute!" she held up her hand to halt his chatter. "Back up one step. Davis Morgan, did you say we are getting married? Is that what I heard you say?"

"That is what I said. That is if you will have me?"

"Not unless you ask me properly," the lady responded. "I have not yet heard your proposal."

Davis reached across the table to take both of her hands in his. "Deidre, I'm not sure that to consent would be the smartest decision you ever made, but my heart will be broken if you say *no*. I love you, and I want to spend the rest of my life with you. Will you marry me?"

There was a pause that Davis interpreted as punishment for assuming too much. Then her face lit up with one of the biggest smiles he had ever seen. "Of course I will marry you. I've thought of little else for days. There is nothing I want more than to be your wife."

People at three nearby tables, who obviously were eavesdropping, broke into applause. "Go ahead and kiss her!" someone shouted. Davis did not recognize the male voice, but he was delighted to comply.

When the happy couple left the restaurant a few minutes later, they spotted Charley and a date on the sidewalk out front. Davis called out to his friend, "I'm glad we ran into you, Charley. I want to tell you the good news. Deidre has agreed to be my wife, and I want you to be the best man when we tie the knot."

"Wow! I knew it was likely to happen, probably before you knew," Charley informed his friend. He grabbed Davis's right hand to shake it vigorously. "She deserves better than you, pal, but I couldn't be happier. Maybe she will be able to improve your disposition." The young police officer then hugged Deidre and assured her, "You could have searched for a hundred years and never found a better man."

When Charley and his date, Debbi, got into the foyer, Charley excused himself to go into the men's room. He went to the sink where he washed first his hands and then his face before he paused to look straight ahead for a couple of minutes. The tough young policeman had not shed tears since his father passed away a decade earlier, and now after all these years they threatened to reappear. He could not let anyone see him cry. He was pleased that she had chosen a good man who, no doubt, would make her happy. He would make sure she never knew of his love for her.

AFTERWORD

Adairsville is indeed one of the garden spots of beautiful North
Georgia. The places described in Davis and Deidre's story are
actual locations we have enjoyed for a long time. It would
be a great place for you to visit if you are among those who love the
uniqueness of small town life. Most of the landmarks described are
still there. The Adairsville Inn, the 1902 Stock Exchange, Corra Harris
Bookshop, City Hall, the big house on Railroad Street, and other
locations are still standing and as charming as described.

The story of skeletons found in the cave on the Ammon property
as World War I raged in Europe happened as reported in our story.
We learned of this incident from the account by the late Alice Butler
Howard (See *Life in Adairsville, Compiled by Danny Pelfrey*). It is true
that the mystery of the identity of the bones and how long they had
remained in the cave was never solved. Maybe it didn't happen the way
our story tells it, but it is possible along with many other scenarios.
Everyone and every part of the story content in *As a Shield*, besides the
discovery of the bones, are pure fiction, but most of the characters are
typical of the people you would find should you visit our town.

The story is not yet complete. Will the marriage of our two heroes
finally take place, and if so what kind of problems will the age difference

create? What about Charley? Will he find the Lord and will he find love? Will Davis return to the pastorate?

We believe it will take at least one more book to complete the story. And it all is sure to unfold in the midst of some fascinating mystery that has roots in the history of the little Georgia town called Adairsville.

Danny and Wanda Pelfrey

Adairsville, Georgia